D0409146

TUNNEL VISION

Bradbury Press ⇌ Scarsdale, N.Y.

TUNNEL VISION

By Fran Arrick

I am grateful to Frederick A. Swedish for technical help and
advice.—F.A.

"The Sheepherder" by Lew Sarett was originally published by Henry Holt
and Co., Inc. New York, in *Slow Smoke* by Lew Sarett. Copyright 1925 by
Henry Holt and Co., Inc.

Library of Congress Cataloging in Publication Data
Arrick, Fran. Tunnel vision.
Summary: After 15-year-old Anthony hangs himself, his family, friends,
girlfriend, and a teacher must deal with their feelings of guilt and bewil-
derment.
    [1. Suicide—Fiction] I. Title.
PZ7.A74335Tu   [Fic]   79-25939
ISBN 0-87888-163-8

TUNNEL VISION

THE SHEEPHERDER by Lew Sarett

Loping along on the day's patrol,
I came on a herder in Jackson's Hole;
Furtive of manner, blazing of eye,
He never looked up when I rode by;
But counting his fingers, fiercely intent,
Around and around his herd he went:

> *One sheep, two sheep, three sheep, four . . .*
> *Twenty and thirty . . . Forty more;*
> *Strayed—nine ewes; killed—ten rams;*
> *Seven and seventy lost little lambs.*

He was the only soul I could see
On the lonely range for company—
Save one lean wolf and a prairie-dog,
And a myriad of ants at the foot of a log;
So I sat the herder down on a clod—
But his eyes went counting the ants in the sod:

> *One sheep, two sheep, three sheep, four . . .*
> *Fifty and sixty . . . seventy more;*
> *There's not in this flock a good bell-wether!*
> *Then how can a herder hold it together!*

Seeking to cheer him in his plight,
I flung my blankets down for the night;
But he wouldn't talk as we sat by the fire—
Corralling sheep was his sole desire;
With fingers that pointed near and far,
Mumbling, he herded star by star:

> *One sheep, two sheep, three—as before!*
> *Eighty and ninety . . . a thousand more!*
> *My lost little lambs—one thousand seven!—*
> *Are wandering over the hills of Heaven.*

1
⇌

Anthony died.

He died in his own house and by his own hand. Anthony's mother thought he must have left for school early, before she got up. It was only when she went into his room to get a stapler he'd borrowed from the office downstairs that she saw him. They were alone in the house, she and her son.

". . . show us where you found him?"

The policeman was asking her a question. She knew it was a question because she heard the rising inflection at the end, but she didn't hear the words. All she heard was the sound of her own voice inside her head saying: Anthony died. She had to keep saying it over and over so that she would be able to believe it and then do whatever was expected of her as she always tried to do. The officer's hand was resting lightly on her arm. She had called the police, she remembered that. She had called and now they were here and they expected something of her . . .

". . . Mrs. Hamil?"

"Yes."

"Can you tell us where you found him? Where he is?"

"What?"

"Upstairs, Ma'am?"

"Oh. His room." Anthony's room. Anthony died.

"Could you tell us which it is? You don't have to come up."

She felt his hand on her arm. "At the top of the stairs, the second door . . . The first door, that's Denise's . . . that's my daughter's room."

"All right, Mrs. Hamil. Thank you."

They left her. She sat on the living room couch, staring at a picture on the wall: two cut-out silhouettes of Anthony and Denise, made when they were five and four years old by a lady at a church fair.

One week before Thanksgiving, Anthony died.

⇌

The two policemen stood in the middle of Anthony's room. The younger one, Officer Lou Consiglia, looked around and sighed heavily. It was so orderly. Neat. A shelf on the wall, filled with gleaming sports trophies; a wooden desk: clean blotter; pencils in a cup on one side with all the points facing up; notepad on the other side—blank; a dresser: comb and brush, side by side; a small framed snapshot of a young girl.

2

Consiglia moved a step to see the snapshot better. Round dark eyes looked back at him from the frame. He continued to stare at the girl, not seeing her face any more, just not wanting to turn back. There was a boy behind him, hanging from a ceiling hook above a tipped chair.

Consiglia's partner, Fred Rudell, said softly, "Come on, Lou," and Consiglia turned around.

"Should we take him down now?" Consiglia asked, also softly. "Or wait until after we search?"

Rudell nodded. "Now. You use the chair. I'll hold him."

"Ties. Jesus, he used neckties. His, do you think?"

"No, give odds they're his father's. Your kid own more than one tie?"

Consiglia said, "He doesn't even own one. He borrows mine when he needs one. Jesus. His father's ties."

Standing on the chair, he cut the tie fastened to the ceiling hook for the light. The fixture, a round globe with its bulb, rested in the center of the neatly made bed.

"You seen a hanging before?" Rudell almost whispered.

"Yeah."

"Last month it was a jumper, remember?"

Consiglia remembered. A nineteen-year-old girl.

3

He removed the knotted remnant and put it on the floor next to where Rudell was placing Anthony. He reached for a blanket, rolled neatly at the foot of the bed, and began to cover the body.

"Fingers are soft," he murmured.

"Yeah. What time is it?"

Consiglia looked at his watch. "Ten. Probably did it between five and seven o'clock. Search now?"

"Yeah, you go out to the car and radio for the sergeant. Then check out the downstairs. I'll stay up here."

"Okay. She say how old he was?"

"Fifteen."

⇌

Catherine hadn't moved from the couch where the policemen left her. Now they were walking around, opening things . . . drawers, cabinets . . . Walking, touching, looking.

"Have you called anyone, Mrs. Hamil?" One of them was leaning over her. She stared at the dark blue of his shirt.

"Called? I called you . . ."

"No, I mean the boy's father?"

"Oh. My husband. He's on the road. In Syracuse."

"Can we reach him? I'll make the call for you . . ."

She shook her head and stood up. "He's at Three Rivers Inn. I have the number. In the office."

"Okay. And can I call your doctor? Your family doctor?"

"All right . . ."

"Anyone else?"

"My daughter . . . She's at school . . ."

"Okay, I'll call the school and have them send her home. I won't say why. You want to show me the office?"

Her fingers flipped numbly through the small leather phone book. She found the numbers, all of them. While he was calling, a third policeman arrived. The first had let him in. They were talking in the hall.

"No medication . . . Just prescriptions for the father, couple for the mother. Nothing for the kids, either of them."

"How about a note?" the sergeant asked.

"There wasn't any."

"Sure?"

"No note."

She shivered. She'd looked for a note . . . something, *anything*. Words from her son, a reason, an explanation for Anthony's body, hanging there from a

5

noose made from brightly colored neckties, his tongue all swollen, a blue tinge around his face and neck. But there wasn't any note, there were no words. When he was little, Anthony was full of words—questions, answers, explanations, stories . . .

"Anthony, this is the last time I'm telling you, stay out of your father's office!"

"Please, Mommy . . . I have to use the typewriter. I have to."

"What do you need with a typewriter, you're only nine years old! You know how your father is about you kids going into the office . . ."

"Oh, but I won't mess anything up! Please? Please, Mommy? I want to make my turtle report on the typewriter. It'll look neater. And it'll be faster than writing all the words with a pencil . . ."

"Anthony, why do you want to write fast?"

"Because it's sloppy when I do it with a pencil . . . Because all of the words come so fast in my head. I can't write them down as fast as they come."

He'd learned to type when he was nine. Behind her back and his father's. Because he hadn't been allowed to use the typewriter in the office and his father couldn't see buying a typewriter for a nine-year-old. Anthony'd learned to type anyway, somehow. She'd never caught him in the office again.

"Mrs. Hamil?" It was the policeman who had been making phone calls for her. She'd left him in the office calling Syracuse.

". . . Sorry, Mrs. Hamil . . ."

"Yes?"

"Your daughter's school says that she was in her homeroom when attendance was taken this morning but she hasn't been to any of her classes."

"What?"

Consiglia sat down next to her on the couch. He looked carefully at her before he spoke. He knew shock when he saw it. He'd seen this face before, too many times, and each time he saw it, he thought of his own boy. Louis, Jr., only fourteen . . . a happy boy, a happy kid, please God . . .

"Mrs. Hamil, do you have any idea where your daughter might go if she left . . . if she skipped a couple of classes?"

She turned her head to look at him but he could tell from her eyes that it hadn't registered. She wasn't hearing him. He stood up and went to find his sergeant, in the kitchen with Rudell.

"That's about it," the sergeant was saying as Consiglia walked in. "I'll radio for a footcop to guard the body until the M.E. comes. You guys go talk to the neighbors."

"The daughter skipped school," Consiglia said. "We can't reach her."

7

"Great," the sergeant muttered.

"We'll go over there anyway," Rudell offered. "Talk to her friends. We'll find her."

"Where's the husband?" the sergeant asked.

"In Syracuse. I left word with the hotel. He'll call here when he gets back, they don't know where to reach him now."

"Great," the sergeant repeated.

"I'm going back in there with her," Consiglia said.

He found her on the couch, in the same position. He sat next to her again and took her hand in both of his.

"Mrs. Hamil," he began, "I have to ask you some things, okay? Could you tell me if your son . . . if Anthony was under a doctor's care?"

She opened her mouth but didn't speak.

"Mrs. Hamil?"

"Yes?"

"Was your son under a doctor's care?" he repeated. "Was he seeing a psychiatrist?"

"No." She shook her head. "No, he wasn't. He was a lot better. He seemed . . ."

"He seemed?" the policeman prodded.

". . . better," she answered.

"Then he *had* been under a doctor's care? At one time?"

"No . . . When he was feeling so low, so depressed, you know . . ."

Consiglia nodded.

". . . I thought maybe he should see someone. But Rand—that's my husband, Randolph, he's a manufacturer's representative . . . he thought it was just adolescence—you know how boys are. He thought Anthony'd get over it. And he did . . . I thought he did . . . he seemed better. We talked to him, talked to the school and everything, we tried to do the best thing, so why . . ."

"Okay, Mrs. Hamil, all right . . ." Consiglia said softly.

". . . But he seemed to come out of it," she said, becoming animated. "He did, *really*. The last couple of days, especially yesterday, yes, yesterday, he was fine, just fine. Do you know what he did? He got up early. Before school. He cleaned out his closet. He *did*. There's a pile of things in the basement right now, right now, of the things he wanted to give to Goodwill, you know the Goodwill? And another pile of things he wanted to store . . ."

"Mrs. Hamil . . ."

"And he went to school and came home with an awful lot of books, he said he had so much catching up to do . . . That's why I thought—You see, he'd let his work slide so, which he never used to do, I mean never, and then the last few months, it just—he just—But last night, he caught up. With everything. And you know what else? He took a shower! Without even being asked!" She smiled involuntarily and Consiglia licked his lips. "Well, I mean, I know that sounds funny, but when he was so . . . depressed . . . he just never seemed to care about showers or clean clothes or anything, Rand would get so angry . . ."

"Mrs. Hamil . . ." Consiglia held her hand tighter. "That . . . that does happen sometimes . . . I mean, the person's made his decision, you see, and feels a bit of relief . . ."

"Relief?" Her eyes dulled.

". . . the chemistry of the body changes. The person gets the energy to carry through what he's decided." He looked at her eyes. "Mrs. Hamil, it's just that I've seen this kind of thing before."

She shook her head. "I knew he was all right again," she said slowly. "Our Anthony, back again. And last night he saw his cousin Carl and . . . he seemed fine with him."

"Mrs. Hamil, I'd like you to give me the names of Anthony's friends, okay? And neighbors. People who knew him, okay?" He pulled a small notebook and pen from his back pocket. "Now you mentioned . . . his cousin, was it? Carl?"

"My sister," she said.

"Beg pardon?"

She began to laugh. "I forgot . . . I forgot to give you the name of my very own sister . . ." She was gasping, laughing dryly, ". . . when you asked me who to call . . . oh! I never even thought . . . oh, oh!"

"All right, it's all right . . ." He put an arm around her, holding her as tightly as he could to keep her from rocking too hard and hitting her head on the wall behind her. "It's all right, nobody expects you to think clearly right now . . ."

"Yes, yes they do!" she cried, laughing even harder. "I'm expected to be clear thinking all the time. *All* the time—"

"What is your sister's name?" he asked firmly.

She stopped laughing suddenly. "Ruth Sheldon," she said.

He wrote it down. "Phone number?"

"555-7256."

He wrote and yelled, "Fred!" at the same time. Rudell appeared. "Call this number and ask for this lady. Her sister." He nodded toward the office; Rudell took the piece of paper and went away.

"I thought of Ruth when you asked about Anthony's friends," she said, twisting her fingers together. "Anthony doesn't—didn't—have too many friends, my nephew Carl was one of them, you see, you asked for Anthony's friends and I thought of Carl but I never even thought of Ruth before when you asked . . ."

"It's all right, Mrs. Hamil, it's all right," Consiglia

11

said gently. "Carl Sheldon was his friend, right? And who else?"

"Well, there was Ditto . . ." she said. "That's a nickname. Because he always follows Anthony and Carl, whatever they do. They call him Ditto. His real name is . . ." She fluttered her fingers in front of her eyes. "I can't remember, I can't remember."

"Do you remember his last name?"

"Bonner."

"Thank you." He wrote. "Anyone else? I noticed a girl's picture . . . in a frame on his dresser upstairs."

"Oh. Yes. Jana."

⇌

Jana wandered down the corridor toward her study hall, looking for Anthony. She hadn't found him all morning. But sometimes that happened. He was a year older and had different classes.

She hadn't seen Denise either, but that was nothing new. Denise was always cutting. Her trick was to be marked present during homeroom so the school never called her house to check on her.

Sometimes Anthony would leave the school building to drag Denise back. Maybe that's where he was, Jana thought. But probably not. He hadn't done that for a long time. He said he was giving up on Denise, she could go do whatever she liked.

12

Jana sat down at her desk in study hall and began to write "A.H." in fancy flowered letters on the front of her looseleaf book. She had just finished a beautifully sculptured "H" and was beginning to draw a heart-enclosed "Jana and Anthony" when she heard her name over the loudspeaker. "Jana Zenek, please?" the voice said. "To the office?" Jana frowned and looked at the speaker next to the wall phone as if she were about to ask why it wanted her.

"Jana?" the study hall teacher prompted. "They want you in the office."

Jana nodded but she didn't move. She suddenly felt cold all over. Her mouth turned dry and her tongue stuck to parts of it when she moved it around. She didn't understand why, but she was used to the feeling. Lots of times, she knew, there was no logic to terror.

"Jana," the teacher said again.

"Yes. Yes, I'm going." She got up and made it from one side of the building to the other as well as down a flight of stairs by touching the cold tile wall all along the way. I haven't done anything, she kept saying to herself. Why do I feel so afraid, I haven't done anything. But she did feel afraid. And when she saw two policemen rise to their feet as she entered the waiting room of the principal's office, her fear actually made her dizzy.

"Jana Zenek?" Rudell said.

"Yes?" It was a hoarse whisper.

"You all right?"

She looked from one to the other. "Why are you here?" she managed to ask. Her throat was so dry the sound of her own voice frightened her more.

"Sit down, Jana," Consiglia said kindly. He gestured toward the bench from which he'd just gotten up.

She sat. "Why are you here?" she asked again. Policemen. Again. Unthinkingly she covered her mouth with her fingers.

"Do you know Anthony Hamil?" the first one asked.

"Yes . . ." She glanced quickly toward the door, expecting Anthony to come in.

"What is it you're afraid of, Jana?" The question was asked gently and answered quickly.

"Nothing."

"Are you sure? You look terrified."

"I am nervous from policemen," Jana answered truthfully.

Consiglia closed his eyes, rubbed the bridge of his nose between his thumb and forefinger. "I'm sorry," he said finally. "We have some bad news for you, Jana, about your friend."

⇌

Jana didn't remember screaming. She didn't remember the ride in the patrol car back to her cottage
at The Rosetrees. She didn't remember the policeman calling a doctor because her grandfather didn't
know one and barely understood English. She didn't
remember the doctor's visit or the injection she was
given. In Jana's mind it was ten days ago. The last
time she had seen Anthony. Really seen him, not the
brief moments in school yesterday, but that awful,
awful time ten days ago. Their last real time
together . . .

"I haven't seen you so much, Anthony," she said
shyly.

He was waiting for her after school, standing on
the sidewalk near the door where she couldn't miss
him as she left. He knew her last class and which
door she always used.

"I know," he said.

She looked at him. His mouth was moving as if he
would say more, but he didn't. So she didn't.

"Let's go over to the pond," he said.

"To walk?"

". . . Yeah . . ."

"All right."

Neither spoke as they walked the mile to Mossback Pond. It was all right with Jana who felt com-

15

fortable with silence. Anthony had usually been talkative but lately he had seemed preoccupied, distant. Jana understood moods like that and did not press him. When he felt better, she would be there.

They climbed over the log fence and walked into the woods above the pond. Jana concentrated happily on the crunching leaves under her feet, enjoying the crisp November afternoon and Anthony by her side.

He stopped walking suddenly and called her name. She looked up questioningly.

"Why won't you ever let me touch you?" he asked. His voice was hoarse.

"I–I–"

"I know you like me."

She was frightened. She nodded. "Yes. I love you," she said. "You are my only and very best friend."

"Then show me. Show me how much you like me, Jana."

She saw there were tears in his eyes as he reached for her, but she gasped and drew back.

"At least let me hold you," he said, and now the tears were falling. "Jana, please, Jana please, Jana please . . ."

She had flattened her body against a tree, staring at him in terror. He put his hands on her waist, buried his face in her neck. She could feel the wet from his cheeks.

She thought she would scream.

16

Anthony sank to his knees and wrapped his arms around her legs. He was kissing her thighs and his hands began to move up, toward her—toward her—

"No! No, no, no, no, no!" She broke away, tore herself away and didn't stop running until she reached The Rosetrees and her room.

Děda hadn't seen her, no one had seen her this time. And she wasn't hurt. Anthony wouldn't hurt her. She kept telling herself she wasn't hurt.

⇌

Denise took a deep drag on the joint and passed it on. This was the third she and her friends had lit up in less than an hour and she still wasn't feeling anything.

"Where'd you get this stuff?" she asked a boy sitting on the fence next to her. "And what'd you pay for it? Whatever it was it was too much."

"You're crazy," he said lazily. "I'm gassed."

A girl said, "Me, too."

There were five of them . . . The usual five in the usual place. An unused baseball field in a clearing behind the school.

"Who brought the munchies?" someone asked.

"It was Denise's turn. What've you got, Denise?"

"Two Baby Ruths," she answered.

"That's *all*? Two lousy candy bars?"

"That's *all!*" Denise mimicked. "And I had to rip off my brother to get *that.*"

"Oh, great," another girl said. "We're going to start cutting you off, Denise, if you don't—"

She stopped short as a twig cracked behind them. Denise was the only one who turned around.

"Oh, God, it's just Stevie," she informed the group. "Here, Stevie, try some of the worst grass ever pushed off on anybody . . ."

"No, Denise, listen," Stevie said. He was out of breath. "There were two cops in the school looking for you!"

Denise said, "Oh, shit."

"What'd you do, Denise?" one of the boys on the fence asked.

A girl laughed. "Your brother called the cops 'cause you ripped him off for candy-bar money, right?"

But Stevie was gesturing wildly at them. "They've been asking everyone in school where they could find you. They talked to Jana and a bunch of kids saw them carrying her out of school."

The group suddenly became alert.

"Carried her out of school?" Denise asked. "*Jana?*"

"Yeah."

A boy got off the fence. "You bullshitting, Stevie?"

he asked threateningly. Stevie was a part-time class cutter. He didn't belong to any school clique and so tried to push into all of them. Denise and her friends, the burn-outs, were regularly in trouble.

"No bullshit. I just wanted to warn you," Stevie said. "I swear."

One of the girls, Liz, slid off the fence but instead of landing on her feet, fell and rolled in the dirt path. The others laughed and started Liz giggling.

"Oh, De-neese, you'll be the first one of us get busted," she cried. "Think of it as an honor!" She clasped her knees between her arms and rolled back and forth.

Denise was off the fence, too. "I'd better go home," she said.

Stevie said, "Yeah . . ."

"No. No, not home. I'd better sneak back into school like I was there all the time. What time is it?"

"Eleven-thirty," one of the boys said.

"Okay," Denise mumbled, "okay. That's English. I can just make it."

⇌

Ruth Sheldon sat close to her sister on the living room couch. She held Catherine's hand and every few minutes squeezed it tightly. She had let the doctor into the house half an hour ago and watched while he gave her sister an injection.

"Cathy, let me take you upstairs to lie down—" she began.

"No! Not upstairs!"

"All right, honey . . . Have they reached Rand yet?"

"What?"

"I said did they reach Rand yet."

"I don't . . . no, I don't think so."

The officer who'd been assigned to wait with them came into the living room and Ruth got up. With a nod toward her sister she motioned him into the kitchen.

"Why are you still here?" she whispered. "I can take care of her now."

"Have to stay till the Medical Examiner comes, Ma'am," he answered. "I can't leave until he signs the release for the body. Sorry . . . You want to call the funeral home?"

"I don't . . . I don't know what to tell them." Ruth tensed. Cathy was in no condition to make decisions, but could she make them for her?

"I could call them for you if you want," the policeman offered. "I could tell them they have to wait for the M.E.'s examination, but they could . . . start the arrangements . . ."

"I—I . . . just a minute." Ruth felt she had to

make the gesture anyway. She left him in the kitchen.

"Cathy, dear . . ."

Catherine looked at her blankly.

"We have to make some arrangements. With the funeral home. They . . . have to be notified. We can take all the time you want, Cathy, but we should tell them . . ."

Catherine's eyes clouded. "No time, Ruth," she said.

"What?"

"Please . . . don't take time. Just . . . just do it. Please. You do it."

"Well, but . . . What should I tell them?"

"I don't care. Simple. Quick. I don't want to hear about it."

"All right, Cathy, all right . . . Shall I call Archway's?"

But her sister had turned away and Ruth went quietly back to the kitchen.

She asked the policeman to call. The Medical Examiner's office had to get the body first for a post-mortem, he said. Then the people from Archway's could come and get it. Ruth panicked.

"Are they going to cut him open? Are they going to . . ."

"No, no, not necessarily," the officer explained. "A post just means taking blood samples and things.

An external examination. An autopsy is something else. A post can include it but it doesn't have to. You know if the kid was on drugs?"

"No."

"Well . . . they've got to examine him."

"She . . . my sister . . . just wants it over with, I think."

"Yeah," he said. He dialed, spoke quietly to someone at the funeral home. "She's in shock now. You understand . . . Okay." He hung up. "He's going to call back in a few hours."

"When we're all feeling better," Ruth said almost bitterly.

"Well . . ."

"I'm sorry," she said quickly. "Are the other policemen going to bring my Carl here? And Denise?"

"Yes, Ma'am, I believe so."

"I have to ask you again . . ."

"Yes?"

She rubbed her forefinger back and forth across her lips. "There wasn't any note? You didn't find a note? You're sure?"

The officer sighed. "I wasn't here when they did the search, Ma'am, but as far as I know there wasn't any note. That's all I can tell you."

"Thank you . . ."

She shook her head. I can't believe Anthony didn't leave something, she thought—*something* . . .

"Anthony! Anthony, where are you?"

"In your bedroom, Aunt Ruth."

"Well, come on, we're all going to Carl's Little League game, so get your jacket and—"

"Please can I stay here, Aunt Ruth?"

She sighed and walked toward her room at the back of the house. She stopped at the door. Her eleven-year-old nephew was sitting at the bridge table against the wall, the one she did her jigsaw puzzles on. Anthony was writing. Again. The tip of his tongue was sticking out of the corner of his mouth.

"Come with us to the game, Anthony," his aunt said. She knew he wouldn't.

"Oh, I can't, I have homework and I have to finish my story."

"What story, Anthony?"

"Just a story I'm making up."

Her husband and son were getting into the car outside. She could hear Carl calling to her. But still she came into the room and sat on the bed next to Anthony's chair.

"What's the story about, Anthony?"

He bit down on the eraser part of his pencil. "I sure wish you had a typewriter, Aunt Ruth." He smiled. "I'd be through by now."

"Can I read it?" she asked. "Your story?"

He looked at her oddly. "You want to?"

"Yes . . ."

"You sure?"

"Of course I'm sure." She had never asked to read Anthony's stories before. She didn't know why she was so interested at that time, but she was. It was a strange feeling. It made her shiver.

"Well . . . I'll let you read it when it's finished, okay? It's no good to have to stop in the middle of something," Anthony said.

Carl called from the driveway. She stood up. She didn't want to leave her nephew that way. She wanted to say something . . . something encouraging.

"Your mother tells me you're a wonderful writer, Anthony," she said.

He put his pencil down. "Yeah," he said, and nodded.

"Goddamn it, Ruth!"—a bellow through the front door.

"All right, Bill . . ."

"Go on, Aunt Ruth. I'll be okay. I'm going to make this the third term in a row I get all A's!"

Ruth stood poised at the arched door of the living room. She couldn't recall if she had read Anthony's story after all.

The office phone jangled; she felt her body jump

wildly. "I'll get it, don't worry," she said, but Catherine hadn't even turned around.

Ruth caught her breath when she recognized Rand's voice.

". . . got your message, hon, and I know what it's for, I came back here to the motel for exactly the same reason you called . . ."

Ruth sighed. He'd assumed she was Catherine as soon as she'd said "hello." Just like Rand, she thought, when he has something on his mind he just doesn't come up for air.

"Anyway, I was in the damned meeting and I realized I didn't have the sales analysis for Rudley and Spear, it's sitting there on my desk, right? Cath?"

"Rand . . . it's Ruth."

"Ruth?"

"Rand, we didn't call because of that . . ."

"What?"

"Rand, please . . . listen now, it's bad news, Rand, very bad news . . ."

"Ruth, for God's sake—"

"I'm trying, Rand, I'm trying . . . It's Anthony. It's Anthony, Rand, he's . . . died. He's dead, Rand."

There was no sound at the other end. Rand wasn't speaking now. She couldn't even hear him breathing. She waited. Then: "Are you all right,

Rand? Are you still there?" and she heard herself sob.

"Ruth . . ." she heard. "Anthony . . . My Anthony?"

She realized she was only nodding and said, "Yes, Rand, yes. Oh, Rand . . ."

"How?"

"How?" she repeated dumbly. And she knew she wasn't finished yet. There was more for him.

"How, Ruth, what was it, a car accident or what, what *happened?*"

"It wasn't an accident, Rand." Tears began to stream down her cheeks as she tried to think. Should I tell him to come home first, we'll talk when he comes home, no, no, he won't have that, I know him, I'll just tell him, I'll just say it . . . "He killed himself. Anthony killed himself."

Again there was silence at the other end and after a moment she spoke his name.

"I don't believe it," he said. His voice was flat.

"Listen, Rand, listen to me . . . Fly home, Rand, all right? Don't drive, please? Rand?"

"I'll drive. I'm leaving now." Toneless.

"Cathy's . . . in the living room, Rand. I don't think she can talk right now . . . but I'll get her if you—"

"No, don't. I'm hanging up, Ruth. I'm coming home now."

26

•

2
⇌

Denise opened her eyes, surprised that she could have fallen asleep leaning against the footstool of her father's armchair. Maybe I didn't sleep, she thought; maybe I just imagined I did. Her mother sat on the couch, unmoving. A still life.

Carl was hunched at her mother's feet. He wasn't moving either. Carl was the only one who cried, Denise thought.

She got up heavily and moved toward the kitchen, toward sounds and movement.

"Aunt Ruth?"

"Yes, Denise."

"What're you doing?"

"Trying to fix us some lunch, honey."

"It didn't really happen, did it, Aunt Ruth?"

Ruth stopped washing lettuce, letting the water run over her fingers, and looked at her niece. She almost smiled, thinking crazily that Denise was again five years old—sweet and curious and tender—

"Honey, I wish it hadn't." She kept her eyes on

Denise's face, watching for it to crumble, waiting for a sign, a glimpse of the child inside. But the girl just stood there, twirling a lock of stringy hair. Ruth turned again to the sink, the running water, the lettuce leaves. That little girl is long gone, she thought.

"How long will it take Daddy to get here?" Denise asked sullenly.

"Well, he's driving. From Syracuse. How long does that usually take him? I wanted him to fly, but he sounded pretty firm about driving . . ."

"Probably has a few *business* stops to make first . . ."

"Denise!" Ruth said sharply. "How can you say a thing like that!"

Denise looked down. "I'm sorry," she murmured. "I'm sorry. I didn't mean it."

"I know. I know, honey. Look, here's something you can do. Slice these tomatoes for me, all right?"

"What's that cop doing upstairs?" Denise asked as she took the knife from its holder on the wall.

"He's waiting for the Medical Examiner. Or something. He's supposed to sign a paper before . . . well, before they can take Anthony."

There was a banging on the kitchen door. It startled them both and Denise cut her finger and cursed. Ruth saw a terrified little face through the parted curtains on the door. The eyes were red rimmed, the mouth distorted.

"It's okay, it's Ditto," Denise said, pulling open the door.

"*Denise!*" Henry Bonner fell into the room and Denise caught him by his shoulders. "Is it true? Is it true?"

Denise said, "I think so." She let go of the boy and sucked on her cut finger.

"Wh-What?"

"It's true, Ditto," Ruth said.

"Oh, God, oh my God, I don't believe it, everybody at school says, oh, no, I was just with him yesterday at school, I just saw him, he was fine, I swear, I swear—"

Ruth went to him and held his face between her hands. "It's true, Ditto," she repeated. "None of us has any answers at all. No more than you. So we might as well all just be here together, all of us who loved—" Her voice broke and she held the boy closely, wetting his sandy head with tears. He wrapped his skinny arms around her and began to sob.

Denise watched them both through narrowed eyes . . .

"Thanks a lot, Anthony, did you have to embarrass me in front of my friends?"

"Some friends, Denise. They'll land you in jail someday soon."

He pulled her by the arm away from the baseball

field behind the school. She dragged her feet, struggling.

"Let go of me, I can walk by myself!"

But he held fast. "I don't trust you. I want to see you walk through that door and right into your class."

"You know what everybody calls you, Anthony? 'Mr. Perfect'! Stuffy, smart-ass, Mr. Perfect Hamil! Who do you think you are, anyway? What's it your business what I do? I hate your guts!"

He stopped walking but didn't let go of her arm. "I care about you," he said quietly. "I care what happens to you. The freaks you're hanging out with are doing a number on you and you don't even know it. I want you to grow up and be somebody. You stay with them—" he jerked his head back toward the baseball field—"and you'll end up on the streets or in jail or in the morgue. Or all of it. I promise you, Denise. They're bad news."

"Well, so are you. Ruining the Hamil reputation with your goody-goody perfect act. Somebody has to show there's an interesting side to the family."

"I get it," Anthony said, half-smiling at her. "This whole thing is to spite me, right? That's why you cut classes and crap out?"

"It's not because of you. I don't care what you do."

"Well, I care what you do."

30

*"Sure you do. Take care of your little sister,
Anthony, then everybody'll love you. Make points,
Anthony . . ."*

*He dropped her arm. She rubbed the red spots
where his fingers had pressed the skin.*

"Get into school," he said quietly.

"You bastard," she muttered, glaring at him.

*He grunted a laugh. "Well, if I'm a bastard, what
does that make you?"*

*She stopped glaring. Her eyes softened and she
laughed with him.*

. . . laughing with Anthony. It's been months
since I laughed with him—months, Denise thought,
months since either of us has laughed at all. Except
when I'm high . . . but that doesn't count.

Her eyes stung and she rubbed them. She didn't
want to remember him laughing, that would hurt.
Remember him the way he was, she told herself.
He'd stopped dragging her back into school, stopped
asking about her friends, stopped caring when she
didn't come home at dinner time. He'd stopped caring for her at all. Screw him, she'd decided. He'd died
for her when he'd stopped caring anyway. That was
when she knew there wasn't anybody who gave her
anything but a negative thought at all . . .

Her aunt dried her eyes at the kitchen table. Ditto
had gone into the living room to sit with her mother

31

and Carl. She stood in the kitchen doorway—a fifth wheel—no one to sit with or be with . . .

"Denise, honey, come over here," Ruth said, beckoning.

"He never cared about me!" Denise cried suddenly. "He never would have done this if he gave a damn!"

"Oh, Denise—"

"He said he wanted to see me grow up to be somebody! What a liar!" Denise turned and ran upstairs to her room.

⇌

The Rosetrees was a two-story colonial house on ten acres of land at the other end of town. It was owned by a family named Corbin who spent only a few days a year there and the rest of their time in New York City and Fort Lauderdale. Jana Zenek and her grandfather spent all their time at The Rosetrees. He was the groundskeeper and the house superintendent. She helped with the cleaning.

In their three-room cottage at the edge of the property, Jana sat up in bed. Daylight streamed over her faded blue quilt, the one her mother had made by hand when Jana was two. Bright and cheering, the daylight was unwelcome. Jana got up and yanked the single drape across the window.

"My fault," she whispered and put her fingers to

her lips. My fault. She didn't whisper it aloud this time but it sounded even louder inside her head.

"Oh, no . . ." A moan escaped her as she rolled back on the quilt. It brought her grandfather hurriedly into the room.

"Janička?" he said softly.

"Děda, I must go out," she answered clearly. She couldn't stay in that room another minute—if another thought, another memory pushed its way into her head she would explode. Ditto and Carl were Anthony's best friends. Carl was his blood relative. They'd be at Anthony's house now. The people who loved Anthony would be there now and that's where Jana knew she had to be, too.

"I'm sorry, Děda," she said in Czechoslovakian. She hadn't spoken to him in Czech almost since she'd met Anthony. She'd suddenly wanted them to be very American. No more foreign ways, she'd decided. She spoke English to her grandfather and he answered her in Czech.

"I'm sorry, Děda," she said again. "Anthony has died and I must be with his family."

⇌

". . . Carl?"

The boy lifted his head slowly. "Hi, Dit," he whispered.

"I just heard . . ." Ditto said. "I came right over."

33

Carl didn't answer. He was still sitting on the floor at his Aunt Catherine's feet. It's like church, Carl thought. The closest he could get . . . sitting at the feet of his dead cousin's mother . . .

"Can I sit here?" Ditto asked. Carl nodded but Ditto was already on the floor next to him.

Ditto raised his eyes toward Anthony's mother. "She all right?" he whispered to Carl. Carl nodded. "Can we talk?" Ditto asked. Carl looked at him sleepily, then looked away. "Please, Carl?"

Carl's lips parted. He took in air, let it out. "Okay," he said softly. "Okay, but not here." He stood up and leaned toward his aunt. "I'm going out in the hall with Ditto, Aunt Cathy," he said. When she didn't respond, he spoke a little louder. "I'll be right back, all right?" He turned and walked down a narrow hall toward his uncle's office with Ditto following. He stopped short of the door and leaned against the wall. "I can't tell you anything, Dit. I don't know what happened."

Tears had filled Ditto's eyes again. "But I saw him *yesterday!* I just can't believe it, I mean, I was just with him! Yesterday at school! He was great!"

"Would you keep your voice down, Ditto, please?" Carl whispered. "I even saw him after that. Last night."

"Oh . . . did something happen—?"

"No." Carl shook his head. "I don't think so. He was in a real good mood . . ."

"You see? He was fine. He was in a good mood . . ."

"So what!" Carl snapped. This kid is so dumb, he thought. How did Anthony and I stand him all this time? Carl closed his eyes. He'd never thought about Ditto being dumb until this minute. He opened his eyes again. "So he was fine yesterday. So he was fine last night. He sure as hell isn't fine now so what difference does it make how he was *yesterday!*"

"Yeah, but maybe he didn't, I mean, maybe it was somebody else who did it." Ditto hopped from one foot to another, scratching his head, rubbing his mouth . . . "Hey, Carl? Maybe it was somebody else that did it?"

"Listen, Ditto, you know how he did it?"

"Uh uh."

"He made a noose out of my uncle's ties. He tied one end to the ceiling thing of his light fixture. He put the noose around his neck and he jumped off a chair. In his room, Ditto."

Ditto's mouth opened and closed.

"Yeah," Carl sneered at him.

"I dunno," Ditto mumbled. "Anyway, it doesn't seem like something Anthony would do . . ."

"The hell it doesn't," Carl said. "He said he was

going to do it. Leave it to him to find a way like this one."

"He never said!" Ditto shouted hoarsely.

"Shut up. He did, you just don't remember." . . .

The three of them were stretched out in the grass above Mossback Pond. It was August and hot, but Anthony was dressed in painter's pants and a long sleeved cotton shirt. Carl and Ditto had been swimming in the pond and were lying on their towels to dry their cut-off shorts.

"Sun's so boiling, Anthony, don't you want to take off your shirt or something?" Ditto asked. Anthony didn't answer. Ditto pulled up a blade of long grass and stuck the end of it in his mouth. "Did you see Lacey Pound and Jennifer Neary down there before?" Anthony still didn't answer, but Ditto laughed and continued. "They didn't see us either. They took off their jeans and shirts and kind of slipped over the bank right into the pond."

"They had bathing suits on," Carl muttered at him.

"Lacey did, but not Jennifer. Didn't you see?" Ditto sat up and grinned at Carl.

Carl stretched up and pulled the blade of grass out of Ditto's mouth. "They both had bathing suits on. Jennifer's was the color of her skin, that's all, I could see it."

36

But Ditto wouldn't stop grinning. "No way. I saw nipples, now you don't see pink circles around nipples through a—"

"If you decided to kill yourself, which way would you choose?" *Anthony broke in.*

Carl slapped the grass and smiled. Every time he and Ditto began one of their fights Anthony would silence it by throwing them off balance somehow. Ditto, Carl saw, fell for it completely. He was frowning, thinking.

"Pills," *Ditto blurted.* "You don't feel anything except high for a little while."

Anthony turned to Carl as if he were a teacher and they were in the classroom. "Carly?" *he asked.*

Okay, Carl thought, I'll play along. "Uh . . . Probably pills. Maybe carbon monoxide. Remember when old man Waylon killed himself in his car that way? The cop told my father he never felt a thing . . . Painless, he said."

"Yeah . . ." *Anthony said.* "I remember that."

Arthur Waylon had lived all of his eighty-six years with his mother. She died on Christmas Eve at the age of one hundred and seven, and on Christmas night, after making out a brief will, Arthur Waylon had gone into his garage, closed everything tightly, got in his car and turned on the ignition. A neighbor, bringing a leftover Christmas basket, had found him the next morning.

37

"What way would you pick, Anthony?" Ditto asked.

Anthony didn't answer.

"What way, Anthony?" Ditto persisted.

"I'm going to do it," Anthony said quietly.

Carl said, "Yeah, sure you are!"

"I'm serious. What difference would it make anyway?" Anthony said.

Carl looked at him, saw that he was smiling. Just a little, but smiling.

"Everybody has to die sooner or later, right?" Anthony said. "Why bother to go through it all, why not get it over with now?"

Suddenly there was loud laughter and a high-pitched squeal from the woods below. A tall girl clutching a shirt to her breast raced up the bank. She was followed by another girl and two boys. They were all laughing.

"See? See?" Ditto cried. "I told you she wasn't wearing anything, didn't I?"

Carl jumped to his feet and watched as the four ran past him toward the dirt parking lot.

"I do remember at Mossback Pond," Ditto said, "but that was just talk, Carl. He was only throwing out ideas and stuff like he always did. It was just talk, Carly!"

Carl winced at the nickname. Anthony's nickname for him. Ditto had never used it. He cleared his throat. "Yeah, well, I thought it was just talk, too, at the time," he muttered.

"It was. Besides, remember the month before that? In July? The tennis tournament?"

"Yeah, what about it?"

"Well, man . . ." Ditto moved his hands in circular motions through the air, something he always did when he had trouble expressing his thoughts. "If Anthony was thinking about killing himself . . . would he give a damn about a lousy tennis tournament?"

"Hey, Dit, keep it down, will you?" Carl pressed his shoulder blades hard against the wall. His eyes burned.

He and Anthony had played tennis for a while in the early spring mornings, but Anthony took it all too seriously for him. "It's just for fun, Anthony," Carl would complain and Anthony would look sheepish and answer, "I know, hey, I'm sorry. It's just that when I'm doing it I forget and I just try to play as hard as I can. I'll be better about it next time, Carly . . ."

But he hadn't been. That summer he'd gone after the ball as if it were his enemy. He never missed it, never.

Carl stopped playing altogether, but Anthony still went to the Colla-Chanca Country Club in the afternoons and played against anyone he could. His father had bought him private lessons and got up early on weekends to take him to the courts—even though he didn't play himself.

Sometimes Jana, and even Ditto, would walk to the club and watch Anthony play. But Carl never went again.

And then, in July, Anthony mentioned the club tournament . . .

"Are you kidding?" Carl snorted. "Me play against you in a tournament? I won't even play against you for fun!" He grinned to show Anthony it was all right.

"I won't even play him Monopoly!" Ditto said.

"I don't really want to be in the tournament. Honest," Anthony said. "But my father wants me to. You know something? I think about it all the time."

"About what, a stupid tennis tournament?" Carl asked.

Anthony sucked in his lips.

"Why?" Ditto asked.

"I don't know. Because what if I lose?"

Carl laughed. "Then you lose!"

Anthony shook his head. "I know. But."

Carl reached over and playfully patted Anthony on the cheek with the palm of his hand. "You know what, buddy? You worry too much. You worry about

grades, you worry about this, about that—Now
you're really getting crazy when you worry about a
tennis tournament! Just think. What if you were the
President with all that's going on now? There's some-
thing to worry about on a grand scale, right? Look at
your petty little worries, right?"

But Anthony didn't smile.

At fifteen he was the youngest member of the
country club ever to win the men's singles champion-
ship.

"I don't know . . ." Ditto said, huddling next to
Carl in the hallway. "Anthony just seemed to care
about things too much to kill himself like that, to just
end everything . . . Even the last couple of months
when he was in such a rotten mood . . . It was just
because he cared so much about everything, right
Carly? Or maybe he just cared *too* much. Maybe you
can care *too* much about things, huh, Carly?"

Carl turned to the wall. "Don't call me that!" he
cried.

⇌

Jana stopped outside the house, staring at the door.
She felt small and very tired, frightened and guilty
and so burdened with grief she could barely stand.
Go in Janička, go little Jana, you must ring the doorbell, she told herself as a mother might talk to a

41

child. But her feet only took her as far as the steps. She held on to the railing with both arms, feeling suddenly nauseated.

It was almost exactly this time last year that she had met Anthony. Only it wasn't chilly like this. It was warm. Very warm for a November day.

She had only been in school for a month. When she and her grandfather had moved from the city in August they had not thought about school, but someone had come to the house and the next thing she knew she was in school again, terrified again of strangers and the unknown. Someone had bumped into her hard, pushing her against the wall. She had screamed and dropped to her knees, wrapping her arms protectively around as much of her tiny body as she could. . . .

"Hey, wait a minute, wait a minute, get out of the way, Dit . . ."

"I didn't do anything, it was an accident, I didn't hurt her . . ."

She heard the voices and tried to cover her ears. When she felt a hand touching her arm she yanked her arm away and buried her face in her lap.

"All right," a soft voice whispered. "I won't touch you again, I promise. But my friend didn't mean to hurt you. He just didn't look where he was going. It was an accident. Honest. Hey. Look at us."

She shook her head and kept her face buried.

"It was an accident," the voice repeated. "Ditto didn't mean it, he didn't even see you. Look. Here's the book you dropped."

"There's something wrong with her, Anthony . . ."

"Shut up. Hey, come on. Open your eyes. Look up. You're all right."

She didn't raise her head, but peeked out from her lap. A boy was kneeling next to her. She saw the legs of two other boys on either side of him. One of them bent down to try to catch her eye.

"I'm sorry," he said hesitantly. "I didn't do it on purpose."

She stood up slowly without looking at them and began to brush off her skirt. But the boy who had been kneeling touched her arm again and she gasped a little, pulling back.

"Anthony, come on, we'll be late," the third boy said.

"You go ahead. I want to make sure she's okay."

She looked at him for the first time. He smiled shyly at her.

"I'm sorry we scared you," he said. "What's your name? You're new here, aren't you?"

She nodded, still looking at him, but didn't answer.

"I'm Anthony Hamil," he said.

She said nothing.

"I'm in the ninth grade. What grade are you?"

She didn't answer.

"Hey. Do you understand me? Is it that you're deaf?" He asked the question kindly.

"My name is Jana," she whispered. He seemed to strain to hear her. "I'm not deaf. I'm in the eighth grade."

He smiled broadly. "Well, hey," he said.

Jana started as a fat man in a shiny brown suit brushed past her and headed up the steps toward the Hamils' front door. She saw Denise open the door for the man and someone standing behind Denise—a policeman. Jana shivered.

The man in the brown suit said gruffly to Denise, "Medical Examiner's office." She stepped back to let him in and was about to close the door when she noticed the small girl crouched on the steps. Denise craned her neck and squinted. "Jana?" she asked tentatively. She saw the girl's face was pale, gray and pale, the color of ashes. Her eyes were so dark and wide they almost looked painted on. Jana stared up at Denise but she didn't speak.

"It's all right, Jana. You can come in if you want . . ."

Jana stood up, put her hands behind her back and

stepped into the house as Denise held the door for her.

"Want some lunch?" Denise asked. "Aunt Ruth made salad and there's soup and bread and stuff . . ."

"No thank you." Jana looked at the floor.

"I mean, there's plenty," Denise said, thinking Jana would turn down a meal if she were starving to death, just to escape talking to someone. "Nobody's very hungry . . . but they're all sitting around the table looking at each other." She cupped her hand to her mouth. "I just smoked a joint upstairs so I could eat a horse," she whispered. "So come sit with me."

Jana lifted her head and stared at Anthony's sister.

Denise wanted to giggle. She knew she'd shocked the girl and for a moment she enjoyed it. Then she felt uncomfortable. "Stevie said they carried you out of school," she said finally.

Jana parted her lips and took a breath. "Denise . . . Do you know why?" she managed to ask.

Denise said, "Because," and shrugged.

"That's not an answer."

"I don't have any answers," Denise said evenly. "Do you?"

Jana put her hand up to her mouth and her eyes filled.

"Come on," Denise said, taking her arm. "Come inside with everybody else."

Everyone except Catherine looked up as Jana came into the dining room with Denise.

Carl said, "Hi." Then he stood up quickly and brought a chair to the table for her. "Want a cup of coffee?"

Jana shook her head, sat down and stared at her hands in her lap.

"It was nice of you to come, Jana," Ruth said.

The policeman appeared at the doorway. "Excuse me," he said, keeping his voice low. "The release has been signed and I can leave now. The M.E.'s going to remove the boy to his office, so . . ."

Ruth stood up.

Jana whispered to Carl, "He is here?"

Carl nodded.

"I must see him, Carl," Jana said.

Carl frowned at her.

"Please. I must see him."

"No, Jana," Ruth said, "you don't want to see him, dear. Remember him the way he was."

"I must, Mrs. Sheldon. It will not make me more disturbed. I need to." She glanced over at Anthony's mother, who was staring at a full plate of food in front of her on the table. Ditto looked up at her with red-rimmed eyes and shook his head.

"In his room?" Jana asked.

Ruth nodded and Jana got up and walked to the stairs.

She hesitated for a second before touching the door of Anthony's room, jumped back as the fat man pulled it open.

"Oh!"

"Excuse me, Miss," the man said. "Just leaving."

"You're taking him?"

"I am, yes . . . For an examination."

"May I be with him? A moment, please?"

"Of course." He stepped out, closing the door behind him.

Jana saw that Anthony was covered by a blanket. She saw his hand was not covered: palm up, the fingers curved slightly. She sat down on the floor next to him and held his hand . . .

"This is a nice room, Anthony."

"Well, yeah, I guess so." He smiled shyly and looked around the room as if he were seeing it for the first time.

"I also have a room of my own." She thought he looked at her strangely. *"I never used to have one."* she explained. *"I had to sleep with my two little brothers. The three of us, we even had to sleep in the same bed."*

"In Czechoslovakia?"

"Yes. I was never in this country with my family.

47

Except my grandfather. My mother and father, my brothers, they had died, you see."

Anthony pulled out his desk chair for her to sit on.

"What is that?" She pointed to a framed certificate on the wall.

"Oh. A prize. For math. I got it in the sixth grade."

"And that?"

"Same thing. English."

She smiled. "You are very smart, Anthony."

"Oh, yeah," he said and grinned at her. Then he sat on the edge of his bed, next to her chair and looked at her. She felt herself blush.

"Jana?"

"Yes?"

"How long ago was it? When your parents died, I mean."

"Four years. And a little more."

"Your grandfather. Who's father was he?"

"My mother's father. He has never really recovered. He used to be so loud, no, not loud, but you know—filled with life. And so funny. But this was so awful . . ."

Jana sat up suddenly. She didn't want to remember any more of that afternoon. There had been so much death in her fourteen years.

Now, sitting on the floor in Anthony's room, with Anthony's hand in hers feeling so cold and so unlike Anthony, she thought of her mother. Not the over-worked, frightened thin woman with bony fingers and shoulder blades that looked like little wings, but the mother with a voice soft as velvet who sang sweet lullabies and funny nonsense songs in her babies' ears at night . . .

It was then Jana remembered what Anthony had said. What he'd said when she'd told him about the change that had come over her Děda.

"Of course he was different, Jana," Anthony'd said. "It would really be hard to get over the death of your own child . . ."

Jana let go of Anthony's hand and stood up. She saw the small picture of herself on Anthony's dresser and she thought about dying herself, right then, right that moment.

A voice called her name and she turned to see Ditto standing in the doorway.

"Come out, Jana," he begged. "Please. The men are here . . ."

She followed him out into the hall. Ditto steered her into Denise's room so they wouldn't have to watch Anthony being taken away.

"I saw him yesterday in school," Ditto said. "He was fine, Jana. I thought he was better than he'd been in a long time. Didn't you?"

"I saw him at school, too, but not for too long a time," she said. "Did he talk to you, Ditto? What did he say? Please? I must know . . ."

"He sounded good! He talked about catching up on his work . . ."

"Did he talk about me?"

"I don't think so. I don't remember."

"Nothing? Think, Ditto, please?"

Ditto frowned and shook his head. "I really don't think so. Funny, because he usually did, you know? I mean, he always talked about you . . . But he didn't yesterday. He just seemed really cheerful. He was in a good mood when I left him. Carl said he was good last night, too. I just don't know, Jana, I just keep thinking something must have happened . . ."

3
⇌

"It had to be an accident, a stupid, senseless accident—" Rand's voice cracked on the last word so that it was almost inaudible.

Denise watched her father from her position on the floor, arms wrapped around her legs, chin resting on her knees.

"I know it was an accident," Rand repeated softly and looked at his daughter for confirmation, as he'd looked at his wife earlier. When Denise said nothing, he turned back toward the mantle and covered his eyes with his hands.

They were alone together. Catherine had finally allowed Ruth to put her to bed and Ruth had left with Carl, Ditto and Jana, after fixing a casserole that nobody ate.

Denise had been stoned most of the day and evening, but now she wasn't feeling even the slightest buzz. With her mother in bed and Aunt Ruth and the three kids gone, she felt a need to stay with her father. The feeling confused her and she didn't like it.

Anger with Rand was easier for her. Needing Daddy came hard.

Rand had not asked her to stay. Until his glance at her, she wondered if he even knew she was there.

"You don't know . . . you don't know . . ." Rand was muttering. "That boy could have been anything . . . done anything . . ."

I know, Denise said to herself. He was everything to you. And now think of all the tennis matches that won't be won and all the A-plusses that won't be earned and the college that won't get him, look at me, Daddy, look at *me* . . .

". . . didn't mean it . . . an accident . . ." Rand said huskily.

"Stop saying that!" Denise cried. "It *wasn't!*"

"How else can you explain it, I just don't understand . . ." Rand looked at her with glazed eyes.

Denise glared back . . .

Crouched over, wrapped in her fluffy blue bathrobe, Denise sat on the second-to-the-bottom stair, listening to Anthony on the telephone. She was only seven, supposed to be in bed, asleep.

"Come on, Daddy," Anthony was begging. "Tell them you can't. Tell them just this time you can't, you have to come home."

He isn't coming, Denise thought, scrunching her shoulders. And he promised.

"You promised!" Anthony said and Denise drew in her breath.

"You have to! She's really gonna cry, Daddy," Anthony threatened.

"Let me have the phone, Anthony." It was Mommy.

"No, just one minute. Daddy, first she was supposed to be Sneezy. But now she's Snow White because Patty DeSylva has to have her tonsils out and if you don't—"

"Anthony, please let me have it now."

"Okay . . ."

"Rand? Honey, don't you think you could fly back? It's so important to her . . ."

Denise, with her chin on her knees, bit her knuckle and left deep purple marks circling the bone.

"I know. I know the ad breaks next week, but your hanging around there isn't going to get the shipment to them any faster . . . Well, but, Rand . . ."

Still crouched, Denise started up the stairs, backwards. On her behind. She could still hear her mother's voice.

"All right. But you promise you'll call her? First thing? Wait a minute, Anthony's grabbing the phone here . . ."

"Daddy? I just thought of something nice, Daddy . . . Last year when our class did Rumpelstiltskin,

Pammy Decker's father sent her flowers. Maybe you could send Denise flowers? Okay, Daddy? . . ."

There had been flowers at the school auditorium for her when she made her debut as Snow White; six long-stemmed roses wrapped in crinkly green paper and a card that said "To My Little Star from Daddy." And he'd called. On the phone he'd said, "I wish I could be there, angel, I know you'll be perfect . . ."

Anthony, Catherine, Carl and Aunt Ruth were in the audience.

When the play was over, she was glad her father hadn't been there. She'd forgotten two of her lines.

Rand noticed the angry look in his daughter's eyes for the first time. "I don't understand, Denise . . ." he began.

"No," she said, "you didn't."

"Wait a minute, wait a minute, are you *blaming*— Are you blaming me—"

"No. No, Daddy, that's not what I was thinking . . ."

"You have no right, you can't—"

Denise stood up. She didn't know *what* she was thinking. She couldn't handle any more and if it was hard for her to be alone, it would be harder now to stay with her father. "I'm going to bed," she told him.

⇌

"Anthony!"

Denise heard herself scream and sat up. She was in her own bed and the room was dark. She hadn't remembered going to bed.

Her eyes adjusted to the dark and she looked around, waiting for Anthony to come in, to see why she'd screamed in the night, why she'd called for him. Then she remembered that Anthony died. And no one came in.

⇌

Her father heard the scream from Denise's room, put his hands over his ears and held them tightly against his head. She's dreaming, he thought. Terrible dreams. I'd have them, too, if I could sleep. When she was little and woke up in the night I'd go in there . . .

"No," he said out loud. I didn't go in, he thought. Catherine did. Or Anthony. Anthony went in to her mostly.

He grabbed for his pillow, put it on his knees, buried his face in it. I was a good father, I loved him, he was a good boy, I had such hopes . . .

He heard himself sobbing. Next to him, Cath-

•

erine didn't stir. Rand eased one foot over the side of the bed. He wanted to go to Denise but then he stopped. She doesn't want me, he thought. She doesn't want to see me. I'm the last person she wants to see. If I went in there, I don't know what she'd say to me . . .

"*Anthony! Phone!*" *Catherine called up the stairs.* "*Anthony! Ditto's on the phone!* Anthony!"

"*He's not going to answer you, Mom,*" *Denise said lazily from the living room.*

Rand put down his trade magazine. "*What do you mean, he won't answer! You go up there, Denise, and you tell him he'd better answer his mother because if I have—*"

"*Oh, all right!*" *Denise snapped. She stomped upstairs.* "*But it's not going to do any good.*"

"*Denise is going to get him, Ditto,*" *Catherine said into the phone.* "*Just a minute . . .*"

It was just a minute, but Denise came down the stairs alone. "*Told you it wouldn't do any good,*" *she said.* "*He won't even answer his door.*"

"*Ditto,*" *Catherine said into the phone,* "*I think Anthony's sleeping up there. I'll have him call you back when he wakes up.*"

Rand took the steps two at a time. Knock knock . . . knock knock knock . . . *He hurt his knuckles* on the wood and cursed. "Open this door, Anthony, it's your father." He waited. "Anthony . . ." Pound . . . pound . . . "You get this door open before I break it down!"

The door clicked and was opened.

Anthony stood there and Rand noticed for the first time how thin he looked. He really looked thin. Rand blinked his eyes. Ridiculous, he thought. I've seen the kid every day this week, for God's sake, he didn't look so thin yesterday. He shook his head. It must be me, he decided.

"Anthony . . ." Rand began, but stopped. He took his son's chin in his hand and studied the boy's face. "What's wrong with you, are you sick?"

Anthony shook his head.

"Well, Jesus, look at the shadows under your eyes. What time did you get in last night?" He asked the question angrily.

Anthony cleared his throat. "I never went out last night," he said.

Rand cocked his head. "Don't hand me that, I was a kid once, too, you know . . . Did you get any sleep?"

"I don't know," Anthony said.

"Yeah, well . . ." Calm down, Rand told himself. He almost smiled. Anthony is just a normal kid, that's all, doing what . . . he sighed . . . doing what *you don't get to do so much when you're older. A normal kid. And covering up for it like a normal kid. "Look, son," he said softly. "I know how it is."*

Anthony looked at him.

"I do, son, even though you find that hard to believe from your old man . . . But listen, kid, you can't go around worrying your mother, okay? You had a phone call down there, she called you, you have to answer her, you understand? Say you're busy or you're tired or whatever, but answer."

Anthony blinked his eyes.

"Good, okay," Rand said, clapping him on the shoulder. "I'll tell her you're sleeping. And that's just what you better do." Rand chuckled. "You look like hell, kid!"

You look like hell, kid, you look like hell, kid, you-look-like-hell-kid . . . That was September, wasn't it . . . two months . . . two months ago . . . Wasn't it?

Rand's face was dripping wet. His hair, his pajamas. When had he put them on?

"It was an accident!" he cried and flung the covers off. They fell over Catherine, still sleeping soundly. Rand felt angry, jealous that she could sleep, though he knew she'd taken a sedative. *He* hadn't taken anything, he was strong enough without that, he'd wanted his head clear . . .

58

He stumbled to his chest of drawers and reached into the bottom one for a clean pair of pajamas. Sweating, he thought. Fever, oh Christ, that's all I need now is the flu.

The bedroom door was ajar. As he straightened to pull on his pajama bottoms, his eyes focused on Anthony's door, directly across the hall. It was shut. Anthony's life was shut. Locked. And Anthony had taken the key.

He couldn't have meant it, Rand thought, the pajama top bunched in his fists. Poised at his door, he listened for any sound from Denise . . . for an answer from Anthony.

⇌

3:30 A.M. Carl and Ditto were also awake. Ditto had begged Ruth and Carl to let him stay at their house, not to take him home to face his nightmares alone. Ruth agreed willingly, Carl reluctantly, though now, because he could not sleep, he was glad to have Ditto with him.

They sat on the floor of Carl's room with incense burning in a tiny pot between them. They were trying to pray. It was the only thing they could think of to do.

". . . and please let his soul rest in peace, God, even though it was a sin what he did," Ditto was say-

59

ing softly. "Because he really was a good person . . ."

"Yeah, he was," Carl interjected. "He was the best person. Maybe that's why he died . . . He was perfect. He was too perfect to live. Good people die young, isn't that what they say?"

"Please, God," Ditto said, looking at the ceiling, "take care of our friend and tell him . . ."

"Tell him we miss him."

⇌

"Hey, Ruth?"

"Hm?"

"You awake?"

"Yes, Bill, I'm awake." Ruth Sheldon lay on her back with her arms folded behind her head.

"Thinking about Anthony?" her husband asked.

Ruth tightened her lips. "Of course . . . and about Carl . . ."

"Carl's okay," Bill Sheldon said firmly. "Anthony was always a little . . . you know . . . off the wall."

"Anthony was a nice, bright, sensitive kid, Bill. You never paid any attention to him. You didn't know him." Ruth stared up at the ceiling.

"He was crazy. What other explanation you got for what he did?"

"Anthony was not crazy. He was depressed."

"Ha! I'll say he was depressed. Listen, Ruth . . ." Bill rolled over on his side to face her. "Everybody gets depressed. Everybody *doesn't* . . . you know."

"You can say it, Bill."

"All right, all right. Everybody doesn't . . . commit suicide." He shuddered.

Ruth felt it and turned toward him. "It happened, Bill. It's nothing to be ashamed of. We can't close our eyes and pretend it didn't happen. We have to face it and talk about it. Especially with Carl."

"Well, what do we do, Ruth, watch him every time he gets depressed? You gonna watch me? I'm gonna watch you?"

Ruth sat up. One of her arms had fallen asleep and she rubbed it, feeling pins and needles. "Anthony's was a different kind of depression, Bill. Most times people come out of theirs. Anthony just didn't come out of it. The pity is nobody realized it."

"Oh, yeah? Well, he did come out of it. Carl said so. Said Anthony was real great yesterday. I mean, day before. Said he was just fine."

Ruth sighed. "I know. So did Cathy."

"Ruthie, do you think I ought to go over there tomorrow?" Bill touched her shoulder gently. He knew what she would say but he hoped against hope . . .

"Yes, I think you ought to go over there, Bill. You should've gone today, you know."

He shook his head. "I . . . can't face 'em, Ruthie. I don't know what to say. What do you *say* to people?"

"Just be there, Bill. You don't have to say anything."

He turned away from her. "I never knew what to say to 'em even before this," he said.

"I know you didn't get along so well with Rand . . ."

"It wasn't I didn't get along with him. First of all, he's not around that much. Because of his business. Then when he was around, what'd he talk about? The country club? And Anthony's tennis scores? And Anthony's swimming trophies? Your sister's husband always made me feel like I should kiss his feet because he allowed me in his house, for God's sake!"

"Bill, his son is dead."

"Yeah, I know. I know."

"Bill?"

"What?"

"Talk to Carl about Anthony. And let him talk to you, too, okay? I think it's important. I have a feeling that Rand just isn't going to face this. Poor Anthony's suicide will be swept under the rug and pretty soon the whole family'll have him dying from cancer or a car accident or something . . . That would be wrong, Bill."

⇌

Ditto watched the ceiling of Carl's room grow lighter but not brighter. The incense in the pot on the floor had burned out, but the smell of sandalwood clung to the room. It made Ditto feel sick.

Anthony would be laid out today—Ditto had forgotten what time . . . He played with a corner of the sheet on his bed. Carl and I, he thought, we never mentioned God, practically in all the years we've known each other. We were never religious . . . But last night, all we did was talk to God . . .

"Dit. You just wake up?"

Ditto turned. Carl was lying on his stomach, his right hand hanging limply off his bed. Half of his face was buried in a pillow.

"I don't think so. I think I've been awake all the time. But maybe not."

Carl said, "Mph."

"What time's the wake, you remember?"

"One, I think. I don't know."

Ditto propped up his head on his elbow. "Hey, Carl, how does that go? That saying—'There is a purpose to all things . . .'—what's the rest of it?"

". . .'There is a purpose to all things in heaven and earth . . .' Something like that, I forget. Why?"

"Because I want to know what purpose there was

to Anthony. To his dying like that. Maybe we're supposed to do something."

"Oh, yeah? We're supposed to do something now because Anthony killed himself?"

Ditto winced at what he thought was Carl's mockery. "Well . . . yeah. I mean if there's a purpose then maybe we're supposed to find out what it is."

But Carl wasn't mocking him. Maybe Ditto isn't so dumb, he thought. "Like what, do you think?" he asked, sitting up.

"I don't know yet," Ditto answered. "But let's think about it. Maybe there was something Anthony wanted to do that he never got done. Maybe we could do it for him."

Carl repeated, "Like what?"

"I *said* I don't know now." Ditto felt unsure. He couldn't remember Carl ever turning to him with a serious question. He had turned to Carl and they both had gone to Anthony . . .

"Okay," Carl said quietly. "Then we'll think about it. And maybe it'll come to us."

"Yeah," Ditto breathed. "You know what maybe we ought to do?"

"What?"

"Maybe we ought to go get Jana. For the wake. So she doesn't have to go alone. Maybe that's the first thing we ought to do for Anthony."

64

It's me who's dumb, Carl thought. Not Ditto. He said, "Good idea, Dit," and closed his eyes.

⇌

Denise had gotten up finally, at five, deciding that sleep was something she was not going to know that night. Rummaging through her stash she realized she didn't have enough grass to roll even one good joint. I can't face this day straight, she thought.

She went to her closet and yanked out a pair of jeans. They were on a hanger clipped together with a skirt that fell to the floor. Denise ignored the skirt.

Liz has some hash, she thought. I know she does, she told me about her emergency supply once when she was stoned. I bet she doesn't even remember telling me.

She pulled on a tee shirt that said "I love you but I'm busy" in red letters across the chest, decided it was inappropriate, and changed it for a plain green one with a cardigan sweater over it.

"Who cares anyhow?" she said aloud as she opened her door and started down the stairs.

⇌

"Rand?"

He didn't answer. Catherine sat up, certain she'd

heard something. The front door? she thought. Has someone come in?

It hit her then. Anthony's dying. She had slept her drugged sleep, mercifully forgetting. Now she screamed from its pain.

Her husband gasped, sitting up instantly. "God, what—" And he remembered, too.

$$\rightleftharpoons$$

Liz's house was across town. Denise walked briskly. There wasn't a soul on the streets. A dingy light, the color of smoke, was creeping over everything, so that even the pretty houses with their neat, still-green lawns looked almost shabby. The Kallenbach house, set far back from the street, had a mist over it, covering the roof and chimney. In front, huge hydrangea bushes, their flowers brown and heavy, were bent low with moisture. Gonna rain, Denise thought. Gotta get back before it rains. She began to jog a little and her thighs hurt almost immediately as she chugged up an incline in the road. You're in sad shape, you fat cow, she told herself. No wonder nobody loves you. "Anthony!" she yelled hoarsely at the sky. "You never told me it was because I'm fat!"

She reached her friend Liz's house panting and exhausted. She hurt all over but she felt good. A little thrill ran through her. I'll run all the way home, too, she thought.

Liz's house was still. Well, what'd you expect at five-thirty, she thought, pursing her lips. Streamers and 'surprise!'?

She went around to the back, to Liz's window. It was a ranch house and all the rooms were on one floor. She knew if she could stand on something, she'd be able to see through Liz's window.

She found a discarded milkbox in the yard near the garage and pulled it over. She stood on it and peered in. Liz was sprawled on top of her covers, her arms flung out, one of them crooked against the wall next to the bed. She was wearing a shortie nightgown that had crept up to her breasts.

Denise stifled a giggle. I should paint 'Welcome Rapist' on her stomach, she thought. That's funny!

She rapped on the window. Liz did not stir. Damn, Denise thought. The stupid druggie's not just sleeping, she's passed out! I'll never get her up. She knocked again, louder, then shrank down, realizing she'd been too loud. Inching up again, she saw that Liz had rolled over on her side. Daringly, Denise knocked loudly one more time and slowly, agonizingly slowly, Liz came to. Her eyes opened part way. She stared straight ahead. She blinked but her eyes wouldn't open any farther. With one finger she absently scratched at a spot on her thigh. Denise rapped on the window again, this time very softly. Liz continued to scratch her leg but finally her gaze turned toward the sound. She stared unmoving at Denise's face framed in her window.

"Open up," Denise mouthed.

Liz put her hands to her face, rubbed her eyes. Then she scratched her head all over. She rolled her body to her left and fell off the bed. Finally, she stood up, came over to the window and raised it.

"Is that the way you get out of bed every morning?" Denise asked with a smile.

"Yeah, it's the only way I'd ever make it. What're you doing here, anyway? What time is it?" Liz mumbled. Her eyes were still half-closed.

"About five-thirty I guess. Look, Lizzie, I need a favor, then I'll leave and you can go back to sleep."

Liz's hand flew to her mouth. "Denise! Oh, my God, I forgot! About Anthony, I mean. Oh, Denise— Hey, look, come around to the back, I'll let you in." She was gone before Denise had time to tell her she didn't want to come in. Sighing, Denise went to the back door.

"Shh. Come on in," Liz said with a finger to her lips. "My room. They'll never hear us."

Denise followed her and Liz closed her door and leaned against it.

"Denise, is it true? You wouldn't believe the

rumors flying around school yesterday after you left. Naturally, most of them started with Stevie—I swear, that kid—oh, jeez, I'm sorry, anyway what did happen?"

"What are the rumors?" Denise asked calmly.

"That Anthony died but that he . . . did it himself."

"Yeah, it's true," Denise said matter-of-factly. "How did the rumors have him do it?"

"Stevie said pills. Roddy said pills. Audrey Ferris called me last night at eleven-thirty—was my father grossed out!—and she said he slashed his wrists. Jennifer, I think it was, said he hung himself."

Denise rolled her eyes. She said, "People are so stupid."

"Well, what was it?" Liz asked.

"Sorry, Lizzie," Denise said. "I'm saving that one. It is true, though. He's being laid out today."

"Hey, kid, I'm—" Liz shrugged. "What can I say?"

"You can say you'll lend me your emergency stash. I've got nothing left, Lizzie, and I can't face this without it. That's why I came over. Please?"

Liz backed away and frowned. "What emergency stash? Who told you I had an emergency stash?"

"You did," Denise said angrily. "Lizzie, I need it. Please!"

"I guess you do . . . I'm sorry, Denise. But look, I

don't know when I told you about that but I used it up a long time ago."

"Liar . . ."

"No, Denise, honest. We have a lot of emergencies around here. But wait a sec . . ." She went to her bed and began to feel under the mattress. "I had some stuff last night that I took just so I could pass out. It worked real fast and I don't remember how much was left. Let's see . . . Here." She pulled out a plastic sandwich bag with three yellow pills in it and handed it to Denise.

"What's this?" Denise asked. She'd never taken pills. The strongest drug she'd used was hash crushed in a water pipe.

"Valium. Five milligrams," Liz explained. "They're my mother's. They're easy for me to substitute with vitamins. My father takes the blues. They're better, they're ten mils, but I can't find anything to put in their place when I swipe them."

Denise held the pills in her hand and looked at them.

"I told you we have a lot of emergencies around here," Liz said with a giggle. "Haven't you ever ripped off your medicine chest?"

"Uh uh. My parents don't take anything interesting. They probably should. Maybe I should save these and slip them into my father's orange juice."

"What time's the wake?"

"I don't remember."

"Well, I mean, a lot of the kids will probably want to go, you know?" Liz said. "Is there a service or something?"

"God, I don't know, Liz. I haven't been to that many . . . No, wait a minute . . . When my grandmother died two years ago, we went and saw her laid out . . . I think it was two days it lasted. I don't remember any service . . . people just came in and looked at her. You know. Then they mumbled something to my parents and just left. I don't think they do anything . . ." She sat down heavily on Liz's bed, still clutching the yellow pills. "I want one of these now, Lizzie. Could you get me some water?"

"Sure." She left the room and returned with a Dixie cup.

"Should I take two?" Denise asked.

"Start with one. If you need more you can have it."

Denise swallowed one of the yellow pills and lay back on Liz's bed. "Oh, God, listen. It's really raining now. I ran over here. Now I have to get back. In the rain! I'll walk in soaked and maybe my parents'll be up and they'll know I was out."

"Tell them you couldn't sleep and went for a walk. After all, Denise, you're entitled to do something zonky after what happened."

"This bed feels nice," Denise said. "Mine is like a rock."

"Take a nap, go ahead," Liz said. "Later on I'll call up your house and tell them you're here."

"I didn't even close my eyes last night," Denise mumbled.

"Yeah, I can imagine." Liz's voice began sounding stuffy. Muddy. Denise fell asleep almost instantly.

4

⇌

Denise opened her eyes at the sound of harsh voices. Her nose itched. Who is yelling like that? she wondered. Where am I?

". . . late for school again, you lazy slob, and what is *she* doing here!"

". . . already told you and will you shut your mouth, you—"

Denise closed her eyes against the voices. Liz. Yeah. Liz's house. Liz's bed, Liz's mother . . . oh, Lord, what time is it? What happened, how long did I sleep?

Slam! Liz's door closed loudly. Denise was afraid to see which one of them had left, Liz or her mother.

"I'm sorry, Denise. Really. I fell asleep right after you did. My mother just woke me, the old witch!"

"What time is it?" Denise asked groggily.

"Eleven, God, I'm sorry, Denise. I never did call your parents."

Denise moved her tongue around in her mouth. It

felt gummy. She sat up too quickly, felt dizzy. She held her head with both hands.

"You all right?" Liz asked.

"Mmmm. Yeah. Those are good pills, Lizzie, but only if you want to be out of the world!"

"Nah, you were tired, that's why it hit you so hard. Listen, kid, you better phone somebody. You'll be in bad trouble and that's all you need now—What time was the wake again?"

"I told you, I don't know," Denise said. She felt grumpy and sick, but most of all, disoriented. "What are you going to do?" she asked Liz.

Liz giggled. "I'm supposed to go to school," she answered.

"Are you going?"

"I might . . ."

"I won't go home if you don't go to school," Denise proposed.

"What about the funeral parlor thing?"

Denise shook her head back and forth slowly. "Can't do it," she said. "I can't go to that. My God, do you think they'd leave the coffin open?"

"Why?" Liz asked.

"Never mind, never mind, I just can't go. Let's do something, Lizzie . . ."

"What?"

"Let's go down to the pond or something. Are you sure you don't have any grass? I don't want another

74

one of these things and anyway I want to save them for tonight so I can sleep." She tucked the two remaining pills in the plastic bag into her jeans pocket.

Liz stood up and began pulling on her clothes. "I swear I don't have any, but let's go over to the school and find Roddy. He'll have some for sure and if I tell him it's for you he probably won't even charge us." She paused. "You got any money?" she asked. "Just in case?"

"Are you kidding?"

"Me neither. But I bet he won't ask for it. You know, because of what happened."

$$\rightleftharpoons$$

"You're not going to school, Janička?"

"No, Děda," she whispered.

He looked at her helplessly, twisting his hands together. "Busy is what helps me," he said haltingly. "If you would like to be busy, you could work with me. On the hedges. In the front, near the gate."

Jana shook her head. "I will go in a while to Archway's Funeral Parlor."

Bohumil Vasulka felt overwhelmed by the distance between them. Little Janička, his baby, his favorite, God had saved both of them, God had saved him to take care of her, bring her to the U.S.A. and stay together always . . .

75

Now she seemed grown up, with another new grief he could not share, going alone to an American funeral parlor.

Man will hurt man everywhere, he thought. I wanted her to have no more hurt . . .

⇌

Denise and Liz sat in the wide clearing overlooking Mossback Pond. They'd moved there and spread out a Boy Scout poncho because the oaks dripped the morning's rain on them when they'd sat in the woods. It wasn't raining now but Denise thought gloomily that it probably would again soon.

She leaned over and touched the end of her roach to a wet leaf.

"What'd you do that for?" Liz asked. "There were some good tokes left."

"It's lousy grass. The same stuff we had yesterday. Boy . . ."

"What?"

"Nothing. I just can't believe it was yesterday, that's all. It seems a million years ago."

"I can't believe it, either," Liz said, leaning back. "You know I had a crush on Anthony?"

"You're kidding!"

"No, I did. Of course, that was before he met Jana . . ."

76

"Yeah. Anthony never even thought about girls before Jana. And then of course he'd have to pick a weird one . . ."

"Yeah . . . I used to think he was so sexy . . . but a little too perfect, you know what I mean?"

Denise snorted.

"Well, I was kind of afraid of him. I mean, he was so smart and everything . . ."

"He should be. He studies—" Denise bit her tongue. "I mean—he *studied* practically day and night."

"No, but—" Liz gestured in the air, searching for the right words "—there was just something about him, I don't know what it was." . . .

"Look at the pond, Denise!"

She looked down and made a face. "It's green. Yucky."

"No," Anthony said, putting a hand on her shoulder. "Don't think of it like that. Think of it like . . . the Yellow Brick Road!"

"It's green," she repeated. "It's got algae all thick in it. You can't even see through it, like you're supposed to with water."

Anthony made a clicking noise with his tongue. "Okay," he conceded, "but look how the green stuff swirls around and around. Like a never-ending road. You could walk on it forever . . ."

Denise said, "It's killing the fish."

"But it's beautiful. I'd like to be very tiny and just walk on all those beautiful swirls, watch the colors change, watch the different patterns . . . Wouldn't that be nice?"

"You'd drown," she said.

Anthony smiled. "But what a peaceful kind of death."

Denise was feeling a mild buzz. She looked over at Liz and smiled. "Yeah, there was something about him," she said lazily. ". . . a peaceful kind of death. Well, he sure didn't pick a peaceful kind. I would've figured he'd drown himself or something."

"Why? What did he pick?" Liz asked.

"Never mind," Denise said, suddenly alert.

"You know, Anthony once wrote an English composition about death. Did your teacher read it to you?" Liz asked.

"No!" Denise was surprised. "Who's your English teacher?"

"Pratt. Who's yours?"

"Lauder. Why did Pratt read Anthony's composition to you?"

"Not just to me," Liz said, "to the whole class. He thought it was good. It was about death, but I never thought anything about it at the time, you know? I mean, it was just a composition, I never figured Anthony was serious . . ."

"When was this?"

"About a month ago. It was all really romantic, kind of. Like death wasn't really a bad thing at all."

Denise looked down at the pond below. "Yeah," she whispered. "What exactly did he say?"

"Oh . . . I don't remember it all now . . ." Liz wiggled around on the poncho and zipped up her jacket. "Something about death seeming so awful to the people who are left, but only for a while, then they realize they're probably better off."

"What?" Denise said, frowning.

Liz shrugged. "I don't know, *something* like that," she said.

"Think, Lizzie," Denise begged suddenly. "It's important. What did he mean, 'better off'?"

Liz took a deep breath and stared out over the pond. "Okay . . . I think it was that the person who dies is finally at peace, so the people who are still living shouldn't be unhappy about it. As a matter of fact, they'd be better off since the person who died probably made them miserable anyway because he was so miserable himself."

"It was a composition about suicide?" Denise asked, her eyes wide.

"No!" Liz said. "It never mentioned anything

about suicide. It just gave us this terrific sense of peace, you know? Like being stoned all the time. Nobody mentioned suicide in the class. Pratt didn't."

"Boy, he must've really been planning this," Denise muttered.

"Maybe . . . Hey, guess what?" Liz said with a little smile. "I've got a surprise for you."

"What surprise?"

"Look!" Liz reached into her pocket and pulled out a small bottle. "Know what this is?" she asked, twirling it around in the air.

Denise smiled back. "Sure. Vodka, right? One of those little bottles you get on airplanes. Where'd you get it?"

"My father collects them. From his business trips. He's got this whole shelf full. I wait until he has so many of one kind that he won't miss it and then I take one. Or two. Here." She handed Denise another small bottle like the first. "I took 'em before we left the house. See, aren't I a good friend? One for me and one for you."

Denise said, "Oh, wow."

⇌

With Ditto and Carl on either side of her, Jana walked to the funeral home with her head down. She watched her feet and tried to keep pace with the long strides of the two boys.

They had come to get her. She was surprised and grateful. But if they had not come, she would have gone by herself. For the first time in over a year, she would have gone someplace alone, without being forced by some authority . . .

"No! I couldn't go on that, Anthony! You go, I'll watch . . ."

"I don't want to go without you, Jana. It's only a Ferris wheel. Look, the roller coaster's much scarier. Please? I promise it'll be fun. You won't fall out or anything, I'll hold you. Come on, please?"

She was terrified, but she did it, for him. She kept her hands over her face the entire interminable time and hardly felt his arm, tight around her shoulders, pulling her against his side. She prayed she wouldn't be sick.

Finally, it was over. She felt the little car stop but was still afraid to take her hands away from her face until Anthony pulled them away gently. Then he helped her off. She was glad her stomach was calm and that she hadn't screamed.

"You didn't like it, huh?"

She tried to smile.

"I'm sorry. I thought you would. With me. I can

protect you, Jana. I won't let anything hurt you." He put his arm around her again and she clenched her teeth against the stiffening of her body.

"What do you want to do now?" she asked quickly. "Win me a teddy bear?"

"You want a teddy bear?" He grinned. "I'll win you a teddy bear."

"Anthony! Hi! Lend me some money!" Denise had come running up to them. "I'm practically broke. I spent my whole wad trying to win a portable radio. I haven't even been on one ride!"

"Aw, come on, Denise, I'm spending for two now," Anthony said. "Jana's never been to a carnival before . . ."

"It's all right, Anthony," she whispered. "I'm happy just to walk around with you and look at the people."

"But I—I want to win you a teddy bear."

"So keep enough for a couple of turns. Come on, Anthony . . ." She watched Denise hopping up and down, a female version of her brother except chubbier, rounder. Denise had the same greenish eyes that seemed to change color with the weather, the same pouty, full lower lip—even the same dark beauty mark, only Anthony's was on his left cheek and Denise's close to her left eyebrow.

She loved Anthony so she loved Denise. Denise

82

seemed to be glowing; it was worth anything to keep
that happy look on her face.

"Let her, Anthony," she said in his ear. "It doesn't
matter. What matters is we can walk here together
and see what it is all about. I mean, what the people
do, at this carnival. I would much rather watch the
people . . ."

Anthony looked at her and nodded. He understood, he always did. He kept looking into her face
while he took his wallet out of his pocket and handed
his sister the five singles he had left. He couldn't have
seen Denise's little skip of joy before she dashed away.

Jana remembered Anthony's eyes. For the first
time since yesterday she could see their green, and
not the gray of the sidewalk or of the November
afternoon sky.

⇌

"I can't go! Cathy, I can't." Rand sat on the edge of
their bed in his pajama bottoms, his elbows resting
on his thighs, his head in his hands. "Oh, Cathy
. . ." His words were muffled by his fingers over his
mouth.

His wife, dressed in a black skirt and dark striped
blouse, quickly knelt beside him and put her own

hands over his. "Please, Rand . . ." she said softly, "be with me." Her eyes were clear and calm.

"Cathy, it was those kids!" He took his hands away from his face, making fists. "Those kids he hung around with and that crazy girlfriend he latched onto . . . They gave him something, I know it, they fed him something! You know that stuff? You read about it, you know what it is—" He groped for the name. "That stuff, Cathy, when kids take it it can drive them to do things they never would do, even— even kill themselves or maybe someone else. You know what I mean . . . Angel dust?"

"Rand . . ."

"PCP. That's it. You know what that can do if you take it?"

"Oh, Rand . . . please get dressed . . ."

"The good kids . . . the ones with the most po- tential . . . They're the ones that die. . ."

He stopped and looked at her. She caught her breath: it was Anthony's face.

"Ruth and Bill have been waiting a half hour in the living room. We have to go now." She wanted to tell him that Denise was gone and had been since they woke up hours ago, but she hadn't mentioned it. She told herself it was because she couldn't bear to add to his misery, but she knew he would grab onto any excuse to stay home, to stay away from the funeral home.

"Get dressed, Rand."

"I can't . . ."

"You have to." She left him staring at the dark suit she had taken from the closet and spread out on the chair. She closed the bedroom door and leaned against it. When had she first realized that Anthony was . . . what's the word, troubled? Not himself? Was it that first time the school called? Catherine rubbed her forehead. Ruth felt something was wrong last summer. But I didn't . . . I didn't really think about it until that first call from the school, whenever that was . . . the beginning of October? . . .

"Mrs. Hamil?"

"Yes?"

"This is Ann Zabriskie at the high school?" She spoke it as a question. She sounded like a student.

Catherine repeated, "Yes?"

"Well, I'm supposed to call if anyone's absent when the attendance sheets come down and Anthony's not here today and we were wondering, you know, if he's home sick." This was not a question.

"Um . . ." Catherine put her hand over the receiver reflexively. Anthony doesn't skip school, she thought quickly. Denise, oh, I know Denise does that sometimes but Anthony . . . Maybe he left to find Denise. That's it. If he isn't in school there's a good reason, I know it . . .

85

"Mrs. Hamil?"

"I'm here, yes, someone just called me . . . Yes. Anthony is . . . here. He . . . has a cold."

"Okay, thank you."

"You're welcome."

Through the day she kept telling herself how trustworthy Anthony had always been. And every kid, she added ruefully, probably cuts now and then . . .

But she confronted him as soon as he came home.

"Yeah," was all he said.

"Anthony, please. This is not like you. Did you get there late? Did you skip the whole day? Tell me, Anthony."

He looked away. He put his hands in his pockets. He seemed bored.

"Anthony!"

"Oh, what difference does it make? I got there late."

"Honey . . . listen. If something's bothering you I wish you'd tell me what it is. I can't understand this behavior, it just isn't like you."

Anthony sighed.

"Anthony, you know how strongly your father and I feel about your education. You have never in your life shown such a lack of responsibility. Cutting classes! I want your promise that this will not happen again."

He wouldn't look at her.

"Anthony . . ." She softened and touched his cheek. "Is anything wrong?"

He wouldn't look at her.

"Tell me. Please. Anthony?"

Slowly, he shook his head.

"Anthony, do I have your promise?"

He sighed again.

"Say it, please."

"I promise."

"All right." She smiled at him. "We'll forget about it."

And she tried to. Everybody always said how difficult kids were when they were going through adolescence, how they weren't little any more but they weren't grown-up either.

Leaning against her bedroom door, Catherine continued rubbing her fingers across her brow.

Rand said it was adolescence, she thought. *And I wanted to believe him.* I wanted it to be true so I didn't fight to get him a psychiatrist. I didn't fight. Oh, God, it was Ruth who first mentioned a psychiatrist. After that day she took Anthony and Carl to the beach. I didn't connect anything or pay much attention to it then . . .

Anthony had wanted to race Carl to the buoy. Ruth said it was too far. Anthony had pushed it, insisting that because he was a champion swimmer he'd have no trouble. Ruth explained evenly that Carl was not a champion swimmer and that swimming in the ocean was not the same as swimming in a pool. But Anthony had issued an ultimatum that he either be allowed to swim to the buoy or she should take him home. It was so odd, Ruth told her sister, so strange, this his-way-or-nothing behavior. So strange for Anthony.

Yes. Catherine nodded to herself. It was. But I remember thinking, everyone has moods . . .

She hadn't moved from the bedroom door.

She thought of the second phone call from the school. I guess that's when I started to really feel afraid . . .

"Anthony!"

He walked past her as if he hadn't heard or seen her coming out of the office and began to climb the stairs.

"Anthony, you come down here!"

He did. But he kept his head down.

"You cut again. The school called." She waited, but Anthony continued to look at the floor. "Anthony, aren't you going to say anything?"

He waved his arm limply and looked away. "What should I say."

"Anthony! I . . . . I don't know what to do!" It was

true. "You made a promise and I believed you because you never, never broke a promise before, but, oh, Anthony . . ." She realized she was almost in tears.

"Mom . . . just . . . just let me go to my room, all right?"

"Anthony!"

He glared at her. "Will you for Crissakes leave me alone?" he shouted and stormed upstairs.

She took a moment to recover before she followed him, caught his door before it slammed in her face.

"Anthony, I want you to see someone. A professional."

"A shrink?"

"Someone like that, yes."

He shook his head.

"You need some help, Anthony, I don't know what to do."

"Forget it. Would you please go out?"

She sat on his bed next to him. "There are people, good people, whom you can talk to. Your father and I—we don't seem to be . . . I mean . . . I'm going to talk to your father about it. I want to find someone!" she finished desperately.

"No."

"Why?"

"Because. It wouldn't do any good."

"How do you know?"

"Believe me. I just know. It wouldn't change any-thing."

She thought he sounded a hundred years old. "Change what, *Anthony?"*

"Nothing! Nothing, nothing, nothing! Leave me alone!" He flung himself face down on his bed.

"Cathy?"

Ruth's voice from downstairs startled Catherine. "Coming!" she called back.

I should have picked him up bodily, she thought. I should have made him go, made Rand stand with me, the two of us taking charge and seeing that our son . . . Oh, but how I wanted to believe the mood would pass. Other kids, they go through a terrible stage, I know they do, but it goes away and they grow up . . .

The Sheldons looked toward her expectantly as Catherine came downstairs.

Ruth said, "It's one-thirty, dear."

"I know."

"Maybe we should just go without Rand? Maybe we should leave him in peace," Bill Sheldon offered.

Ruth ignored that. "Why don't you go up there, Bill?" she said, touching his arm.

"Yes, Bill, that's a good idea." Cathy looked at him, pleading. "He won't say he can't to you."

Bill sighed and got up. He could feel the women's

eyes on him as he climbed the stairs—the same eyes, those sisters, dark and round. But Ruth's had a glint, while Cathy's just looked watery.

He knocked on his brother-in-law's door. Rand didn't answer, so Bill opened it a crack.

Rand was sitting on the bed staring at the chair.

"Hey, Rand?"

"I'm not going, Bill . . ."

"Hey, look . . . you gotta go." Bill was embarrassed. Who says he has to go? Maybe he shouldn't go if he can't take it . . . It's just 'what people think' that makes you go to these things, anyway. Who cares what people think?

Bill knew if it had been Carl he couldn't have faced anybody. He was confused and so he took a stand.

"I'll help you get dressed," he said firmly.

Rand watched as his brother-in-law reached for the clean underwear Cathy had put on the chair next to the suit. Underwear. It reminded him . . . A month ago? Five weeks? . . .

"When was the last time you changed your underwear, Anthony!"

The boy didn't even look at him.

"I said, when did you last change your underwear? Do you know or care that you stink? *Do you know that? Do you?"*

91

Anthony sighed.

"Don't you feel grubby? Sitting around this filthy room in that filthy underwear?"

Anthony's expression was blank. "I don't feel anything," he said.

"What the hell's wrong with you lately anyhow?" Rand cried. "What is it, some girl? That girl giving you trouble? Come on, kid, there's a million others out there. You're only fourteen years old, for God's sake!"

Anthony looked at him. "Fifteen," he said.

"Oh, right, how time flies . . ."

". . . when you're having fun . . ."

"What?"

Anthony said, "I'm tired. I'm gonna sleep."

"Listen, that girl is crazy. I haven't seen all that much of her, but I know crazy when I see it and believe me, she's it. She looks at you like any minute she expects you to hit her or something . . ."

"Jana?" Anthony asked as if it were the first time he'd heard the name.

"Well, who the hell else would I be talking about?"

"I'm going to sleep for a while . . ." Anthony said.

"Anthony, look . . . you're a terrific kid. You always were a terrific kid. Your mother and I, well, we're counting on you. Anthony? Snap out of it, huh?" Rand touched his son's shoulder. The gesture *felt awkward to him. "It's just a girl, right? Can't get that way over a girl. I know how it is . . . Come on, kid . . . Change your underwear . . ."*

⇌

Downstairs, Ruth and Catherine sat together on the couch. Both of them looked up at the ceiling as if they could see Rand and Bill in the bedroom above.

Finally, Ruth glanced over at her sister. "Mr. Archway said it's unusual to have all the arrangements made so quickly . . ." An autopsy hadn't been required, but then Ruth had never mentioned that possibility to her sister. Twice during the previous evening she'd spoken to the funeral director. He hadn't seemed pushy but he needed to know: Did they want the funeral at a church or at the funeral home? Did they want a closed casket? Did they want any sort of announcement in the newspaper? Which minister, the duration of the wake, flowers or donations or both . . .

She had given up consulting Cathy. She herself decided against flowers and directed that if anyone asked, donations should be sent to a suicide prevention center. She felt that was the right decision. She never asked Rand. There was to be a closed casket. The wake would be only one day.

"We're both denying it happened, aren't we?"

93

Catherine asked suddenly. Ruth started. "Aren't we? I mean, there's Rand up there, he won't even go . . . And I just want it over . . ."

"That's normal, Cathy," Ruth said tenderly, wondering what "normal" was.

"I'm glad you . . . I mean, thank you for taking over, Ruth . . . Archway's, and everything . . . That man who was here yesterday afternoon, was that Mr. Archway?"

"No, dear, that was the man from the Medical Examiner's office."

"Oh. Why was he here?"

"It doesn't matter, dear. Everything's been taken care of. Ah, here come Bill and Rand . . . Denise is going to meet us there?" Ruth hadn't thought to ask about Denise before. She assumed the girl would be with the boys and Jana.

Cathy whispered, "I don't know where Denise is."

5

⇌

The closer they got to Archway's, the slower Ditto walked. Jana and Carl slowed down, too, pacing themselves with him. Once he saw the large, white, shield-shaped sign in Old English lettering about a block and a half away, Ditto stopped walking altogether. Carl and Jana were several yards ahead before they realized he wasn't with them. Jana turned and came back.

"I just realized," Ditto said to her.

"What is it?" she asked softly.

"He's dead," Ditto answered.

Carl, hearing him, blew out his breath loudly, shook his head, and looked down at his feet.

"No, I mean," Ditto said, ". . . just for a while I wasn't thinking, you know? We were just walking along, *going* someplace. Just the three of us. And then it hit me that when we get to where we're going . . . It hit me what we're going *for,* you know what I mean?"

"I knew what we were going for," Carl replied, not looking at him.

"I guess I just didn't, really," Ditto said, and thought, I should have done something two weeks ago . . . when I had the chance . . .

"Don't turn on the light, Ditto!"

"Why not?"

" 'Cause I just like it like this."

"Oh. Okay . . ." Ditto stood in the doorway of Anthony's room feeling strange again. He didn't like the feeling. He had always been comfortable—more comfortable—in Anthony's room than almost anywhere else. Especially when they were alone as they were now.

"Your mom said it was okay to come up . . ." he said hesitantly. And when Anthony didn't answer, he asked, "Was it? . . . You want me to go?"

"I don't care . . . You can stay . . . Just don't turn the light on."

Ditto went to the bed where Anthony was propped against the headboard and sat down at the foot of it.

"Your eyes bothering you?" Ditto asked, hoping that was it.

No answer.

"Want me to get you something?"

It had been dusk when Ditto arrived, now it was almost dark. He could just see Anthony shake his head slowly.

"I wanted to ask you a couple of things," Ditto said. "You never go to swimming practice any more . . ." He looked at Anthony's face but couldn't see his expression. "The coach is worried, you know. Because you never skip . . ."

Anthony turned his head toward the dark window.

"Your mother said you were being grounded," Ditto went on. "I asked her why and she said to ask you. How come?"

"I cut school again, they called, my mother found out, she told my father when he called, he yelled, they decided I should be grounded. Okay?"

"What'd you do it for? Denise or something?"

"Denise doesn't know . . . She doesn't know what I do. Or care. Denise is Denise."

Ditto wanted to say I care but he thought he'd sound stupid. Instead, he said, "Well, should I tell the coach you're grounded? Or what?"

"Tell him what you want."

Ditto wanted to ask Anthony why he'd cut school. It would have to have been for a very special reason. Anthony'd never cut unless it was really important. Ditto made a face in the dark. Bet he told Carl, Ditto thought jealously, then swallowed the thought. I'm just lucky he's my friend at all, he mouthed silently, My best friend.

"Hey, Anthony, can you help me with something?"

"What?"

Ditto began to babble. "My sister came home last night and said they need a busboy over at Colla-Chanca? And it pays three dollars an hour but the tips are great because the waitresses really help you out? And now they've got a piano player in there, you know? So it's really packed just about every night, even during the week? So anyway, she offered me—well, she didn't offer me, but she said I could probably get it, the job, right? But if I take it, I probably have to start work at around four-thirty and probably work till nine or something like that, so it'd be awful tough on school work and I'd definitely have to quit managing the swim team. But I sure could use the money and I don't know what I should do."

Anthony's face was still turned toward the window.

"So what do you think? I really need your advice, Anthony, I swear, there's nobody else's answer I'd really trust, you know?" Ditto crossed his fingers that the real Anthony would come out of there, wherever he was, and be his best friend again, solve all his problems by talking them out with him, looking at *the problem from all sides, like a dog worrying a bone until it was mush and sticks. Whatever Anthony said it would be comforting, Ditto knew. Either, "Don't quit the swim team, we need you too much" or "I'd really miss you, Dit, but don't worry about the school work because I'll help you with that," or something.*

What Anthony said was, "Shit, I can't even solve my problems, Ditto. What do you expect me to do with yours? Cram it, Ditto, get out of here . . ."

Ditto left Anthony's room and Anthony's house without saying goodbye to Anthony's mother. He cried as soon as he hit the street, the tears streaming over his cheeks as he leaned against the skinny young oak tree inside the bricked circle next to the sidewalk. I'm so dumb, he kept whispering to himself as he slapped at the tears with the back of his hand. I'm so dumb, why does he even bother hanging around with me. Maybe he won't any more. I better stop behaving like a baby with my stupid questions, I don't blame him for finally getting fed up with me . . .

. . . I should have done something. I should have done something!

"Ditto," Jana whispered.

He looked at her. Carl was still several yards ahead, standing with his hands in his pockets.

99

"Jana . . . Anthony was in a bad way. I mean a couple of weeks ago, one of the last times I was really alone with him . . . he behaved so, he was . . ."

Jana was searching his face. It made him uncomfortable but he didn't look away from her.

"I think I should have done something, Jana. All I did was feel sorry for myself. I just thought about myself—that Anthony was fed up with me and I wasn't gonna be allowed to be his friend any more, you know? I was just thinking of me, not that there might be something really wrong with Anthony. I could never think anything could be wrong with Anthony. Don't you think I should have done something? To help him?"

Jana startled him by her sudden intake of breath. She turned and ran, past Carl, down the street toward the white sign.

"Wasn't that Jana, Henry?"

Ditto jumped again at the sound of the voice behind him. "Uh. Yeah. Hullo, Mr. Pratt." Anthony's English teacher.

He and Ditto began to walk toward Carl, who was watching Jana run ahead, her hands raised and waving wildly near her ears.

"Carl?"

"Hello, Mr. Pratt."

Walter Pratt was a young man, the youngest teacher in the school, and the students liked him.

"You going to the—to Archway's?" Ditto asked.

"Yes. Let's walk together." Pratt put a hand on Carl's shoulder. "I know you were Anthony's closest friends. I cared for him very much, too. I came to feel close to him through his . . . stories and essays."

He'd had Anthony in class last year, asked for him again. The boy wrote three papers for every one assigned. Could have developed into—

"Yeah, Anthony always liked writing," Carl said.

"He had a talent. And such enthusiasm. This last month or so . . . well, I thought it was . . . just something he had to go through. You know? I didn't want to pressure him, to make him think I was on his back . . ." He stopped talking. He thought he must sound foolish, apologizing to these boys. They were embarrassed, both looking at the ground. "Um . . . wasn't that Jana who just ran by here?" he asked to change the subject.

Carl ignored the question and turned toward Ditto. "What happened to her?" he asked.

"I don't know. She just . . . ran away."

Carl shook his head. "She's really weird," he said.

Pratt said, "I know Anthony truly liked Jana. Loved her, I guess. He wrote about her. Some of his best poems were about her. Many of them concerned her life as a little girl in Europe."

"I don't know much about her life there," Carl said. "She never talked about it to me. I never asked her, though. I guess it did a number on her because she does some really wacko things."

They had reached Archway's. Jana was nowhere in sight. The two boys and the man made no move to go up the walk toward the door.

Suddenly, Pratt reached out and grabbed Ditto's arm. "Henry, do you remember Anthony's essay about death? Did I read it to your class?"

"No, Mr. Pratt."

"I did read it to at least one class, I remember . . . I've reread it several times since yesterday," the teacher said, struck by the realization: I never thought it was anything but hopeful . . .

"Mr. Pratt?"

"Yes, Anthony?"

"I'd like to talk to you, Mr. Pratt."

"Is something wrong?" Anthony was glaring at him.

"Well, yes, you could say that. A kid just told me you read my essay in one of your classes."

Pratt offered a little smile. He thought, is that all. "The one on peace! Yes, I did, Anthony. It was quite expressive—"

"You really had no right to do that. You should have asked me first. That was a terrible thing to do, Mr. Pratt."

"Hey, Anthony—"

102

"It was an invasion of privacy!" Anthony began to shout. "It was! You think a psychiatrist or a priest or a lawyer would go around exposing somebody's thoughts in public? I thought it's supposed to be the same with a teacher!"

"Anthony, believe me, I never thought—"

"No, you didn't!" Anthony began to rub his fingernail back and forth across his lower lip. "You sure didn't think! I'm never writing anything for you again!"

As Anthony began to run out of the room, Pratt leaped toward him and caught him by both shoulders, whirling him around.

"Look, Anthony!" He began loudly but when he was sure the boy had relaxed slightly, he lowered his voice and eased his grip. "I'm sorry! I'm sorry. I had no idea it would be an invasion of privacy for you. It was an example, that's all. Something expressive for the kids to strive for in their writing. And I didn't think you were divulging anything personal. If I had thought that, I wouldn't have read it. You tell me what was so personal in there. Please? Will you do that?"

As Anthony look at him, he felt the anger fade in the boy's eyes, so he went on.

"Was it the paragraphs about your grandmother? Because that's the only part I can recall where you even used the first person. She'd been very sick,

103

right? And suffering? And you wrote—wait a minute, I've got it here." He moved to his desk and extracted a file. "Okay, it's . . . here. You say, 'It was as if we had cut the moorings on a cloud-boat, at last allowing it to drift off on its own, floating down a never-ending river of stars; and the rest of us, remaining, must surely celebrate that for her, the ties to earthly anguish are broken forever and she is free.' Now, Anthony, that's a lovely way to accept the passing of someone who had been suffering and had no hope."

Anthony was still staring at him, but without anger.

"Besides, Anthony, we all must experience the death of a loved one at some point and if we can begin to look at it in the way you do here—"

Anthony frowned; the teacher felt he must qualify what he'd said.

"Anthony, look. Your grandmother wasn't going to get better, was she?"

"No."

"Well, you accepted that and wrote in a moving way that she would no longer have to endure pain, either physical or mental. And that those who loved her should remember the good things and be grateful that she's no longer suffering. Right?"

"Yes."

"Well, I just wanted the kids to get that. Under-stand?"

"Yes."

"Are you still angry with me?"

"No."

Pratt smiled. "I'll ask you from now on before I read anything of yours aloud. I promise, Anthony."

Anthony nodded, turned and left the room.

The teacher sighed. Well, he thought, leaning back in his chair, that was certainly an uncharacteristic display. Kids! He puffed up his cheeks, letting the air out slowly. Probably figured it'd compromise his masculinity to let his friends know he could feel something poetic.

I thought I convinced him, Pratt told himself. "Let's go in," he said to the boys. He and Ditto started up the flagstone walk to Archway's door. Carl held back, then followed, careful not to step on any cracks.

⇌

Bohumil Vasulka continued to trim the hedges for some minutes after his little Janička ran past him toward their cottage, her hands holding her face. He thought: to leave her alone would be best; I can do

105

nothing; each of us handles grief as he handles it. But in the end he sighed, and carrying the heavy, old-fashioned, hand-held clippers with him, he followed after her.

She lay, face down, on her bed. But there were no shaking shoulders, no sobs. She made not a sound. He thought she was barely breathing.

He sat next to her and she rolled a little toward him as his weight tipped the mattress, but she did not look up.

"Janička, when your mama died . . ." he began, but he did not know how to continue. He felt the pain, sharp as ever, whenever he thought of it. But in the beginning, right after it happened, there was no pain. There was only fear. He had a goal to reach, the goal of getting over the border, and the fear of not reaching it was all he felt. Remembering this, he began to speak again.

"Do you remember, Janička, when we were in the truck, you and I? And the others had been killed by the gunfire of the border guards?"

She nodded. He couldn't see her face because the side that was not buried in the pillow was covered by her hand.

"I knew I had to cross the Dunaj—the bridge, I had to get you over the bridge, that was all I thought. I did not think about the four people I loved who were lying probably wounded, maybe dead, in the back of the truck. I did not think of anything except reaching the border. What did I tell you then? In the truck."

She spoke through her hand. "To get down. On the floor. To make myself very small."

"Yes. And you stayed there. Long after we were safe, after we got through. We had to pull you out from the truck, from the crouched position, you stayed that way, remember?"

She nodded.

"You did not cry, Janička, you never cried. You were only ten years old but you never cried. I knew you cried inside . . ."

She nodded again, harder.

"Yes, I knew that. And then, in New York City—" He stopped when he felt her violent shudder, then spoke again. "In New York, I did not see you cry. I think perhaps it hurts more when you hold your grief in your mind."

She sat up then but she did not look at him. She stared at the wall in front of her at the head of the bed. "But you weren't responsible," she whispered.

"Responsible?"

"Their deaths weren't your fault."

"Ahhh, Janička," he moaned, "why do you talk of fault?"

She didn't answer him, but shook her head back and forth, closing her eyes.

"I think of fault all the time, did you know that?" he asked.

She continued to shake her head.

"Yes. I do. Who do you think worked on that truck? To make it safe from bullets? Night after night, working, hammering, stealing the metal, the tools . . ."

"Papa did," she said softly.

"Papa and *I*," he corrected. "And the bullets went through the rear doors as if they were made of tin."

"But you didn't know," she told him. "You tried. You did your best. You and Papa thought it was safe."

"I don't understand, Janička . . ."

"With Anthony—I could have made him not want to die. But I didn't. I failed him. It is my fault he is dead."

"Oh, no, Janička . . ." he moved to hold her, touch her. She felt it and shrunk away and he stopped. "You couldn't have helped, tell me how you could have helped? How did you fail your friend Anthony?"

But she only shook her head, holding herself tightly as if she were cold.

⇌

108

"Lizzie . . . I have never been so awful wr-wrecked!" Denise screamed with laughter and flung away the small bottle that had once contained a shot of vodka.

"Booze and grass. You can't beat it," Liz giggled. "I should've taken another bottle."

"No," Denise said, flopping back on the poncho, "I couldn't be higher than I am now. Couldn't. Couldn't!"

"We didn't eat anything," Liz said. "Hope we don't get sick. Think we'll get sick?"

"I don't care . . ."

"What about your parents?" Liz's speech was slurred and she wasn't facing Denise, so Denise didn't hear her.

"What?"

"I said, what—about—your—pa-rents? And the wake? And all that?"

Denise said, "What wake?" and they both giggled loudly.

"Oh, my God," Denise said suddenly, slapping Liz on the back. "Do you know what I just remembered?"

"What?"

"The trophies."

"The . . . what?"

"Anthony's trophies." Denise wasn't laughing any more and her speech was clear. She lay on her back looking up at the sky.

"His swimming trophies?" Liz asked, turning to her. "What about them?"

"He asked me to take care of them."

Liz was staring at her now, but she seemed to fade in and out of Denise's consciousness. Those trophies. It just hadn't registered. But it was months ago . . .

Crash!

The sound of metal objects slamming together, then falling. Great heavy thumps against the ceiling above her. Denise had been sleeping on the living room couch and woke with a pounding heart. Another thump. And another. She put her hand to her throat. Another thump and the sound of whatever it was rolling, rolling, and crashing into something else.

No one was home except herself, and Anthony . . .

She raced upstairs. He was standing in the middle of his room with all his trophies and cups strewn about. Some were on the bed, most on the floor. The walnut-stained shelf, which he had made himself to hold them, was off its brackets.

"Anthony?" Denise said hesitantly. "What happened?" She looked from the mess to her brother's face, then back to the mess again.

110

"Nothing. The shelf broke," Anthony answered. He was just standing there.

Denise picked up the shelf. "It's not broken," she said. "And the brackets are still on the wall." She touched them. "This couldn't have just fallen, Anthony . . ."

"Well it did," he said.

She was about to make a sharp remark to him, something good and nasty, one of her best, but she didn't. She stopped herself by actually putting her fingers over her mouth. Then she said, "Look, I'll help you pick it all up."

"I don't want your help and I don't want it picked up," he said in a flat tone.

It was the first time in a long while that Denise had offered help to Anthony. Always it had been the other way around. His rejection stung.

"What's bugging you, big brother? Have a fight with your crazy Czech-o?"

Anthony flung out his hands in a gesture of exasperation and walked to his window, resting his forehead against the glass.

"Is it Jana?" Denise asked, serious now.

Anthony shook his head slowly, rubbing it against the window pane.

"Hey, Anthony . . . I know how you feel," Denise began.

Anthony said, "The hell you do."

"No, I do, believe me," Denise insisted. "Anthony, listen, it's me. It's not like I was Daddy or Mom or a teacher or somebody. I'm a kid, too, don't forget! I know what it's like to feel so low that you just want to die or something . . ."

Anthony turned and looked at her.

"I do, honest!" she said for emphasis.

Anthony said, "You don't know how I feel, Denise."

"Sure, I do."

"No, you don't! You don't! You don't!" He bent down suddenly and picked up two gold cups. "They're yours," he said, holding them out to her. "All of 'em."

"What?"

"All this stuff—" He waved his arm toward the spilled trophies. "You keep it. And take the polish, too. Clean 'em up, Denise, it'll give you something to do."

She smiled tentatively. "You're giving 'em to me? Are you kidding?" Of course he's kidding, she thought. A weird joke like the ones they used to play on each other a lifetime ago. He was playing! Denise couldn't even remember their last silly, playful game. But she was ready now to pick it up again. "Hey! Big Brother! I can have all these?"

112

Anthony looked at her and nodded.

"Good, because I know just what to do with them . . ." She bent down for a small gold cup. Beginning to giggle, she raced out to the bathroom they shared across the hall. She filled the cup with water and tiptoed back into Anthony's room.

"Hi-i," she sang, the cup behind her back. "See you haven't picked up the trophies yet. You really want me to take them? Last chance . . ."

"Take 'em. Get 'em out of here!" Anthony cried.

Denise reached toward him and poured the water over his head. "That's what I'll use 'em for, Anthony!" she chortled. "Ho, ho, you've sealed your own doom!" Still giggling, she turned and raced out of the room. At the foot of the stairs she ducked into a tiny alcove, figuring Anthony would be so mad he'd be after her in a minute.

She crouched down, pressing a hand to her mouth to stop her giggles. She listened to his heavy step on the stairs above her. Ooh, here he comes, she thought, drawing in her breath, he won't see me, he won't, he'll go right past . . .

Then she heard the front door slam.

"Well, so what happened?"

Denise looked from the milky gray sky to Liz's face.

"What happened, Denise?" Liz asked again and Denise realized she must have been speaking. She hadn't been aware of that—she thought the trophy memories were just pictures bumping against each other inside her own head.

"Nothing happened. I put all the cups back on the shelf and that was the last I thought about it."

"So you never took them. I mean, you never took him up on his offer. That you could keep them, I mean."

"No, how could I keep them? They were his. He won them."

Liz lit the end of the last of their joints, inhaled as deeply as she could, and held her breath. She spoke while she exhaled, her voice sounding forced. "Well, they're yours now, kid. He wanted you to have them . . ." She didn't hear the footsteps in the grass behind her as she handed the joint to Denise.

But Denise had fallen asleep.

"Hey." Liz was so stoned herself that she didn't even jump when she felt the hand on her shoulder. "S'posed to be in school, aren't you?"

A cop, she thought, without turning around. Wonderful.

"Not today," she mumbled. "It's a special day. My best friend's brother died." She looked up then as the policeman took the joint from between her fingers and dropped it onto the damp ground, next to five other roaches and Liz's empty little vodka bottle.

The officer looked for the first time at Denise, sleeping peacefully.

"Oh, God, the Hamil kid," he said out loud.

Liz looked questioningly at him.

"I took her home from school yesterday. I know what happened," he said.

"Oh. Yeah. I remember."

He thought a minute and bit his lower lip. "What's your name?" he asked Liz.

She looked down at the ground.

"Come *on*," he said. "Don't make me get mad. I could get it anywhere."

"Liz. Elizabeth. Keyserling."

"Well, look, Elizabeth Keyserling, you're a very lucky girl. Because if I didn't know firsthand what was going down with your friend here, I'd take you in and book you, Elizabeth Keyserling. I would, do you believe me?"

"Yes . . ."

"As it is, I'm just taking you in." He reached for Liz's arm and pulled her up. "Come on now. Wake your friend."

"Aw, look . . ." Liz said, "she needed something after what happened. You know? Hey, you can understand that, right?"

"Not *that*, she didn't," the officer said, picking up the bottle and skinny little butts. "And neither did you. I think what she needs is her family."

"I think you don't know nothin'," Liz said.

6

⇌

Carl stood alone in the doorway of the small room that held Anthony's coffin: alone as he'd wanted—Ditto and Pratt had turned down the hall. His thoughts were far away so he jumped when his mother touched him.

"Carl, is Denise here?" she asked. His Aunt Cathy was looking anxiously beyond him into the room.

"Uh, no. I haven't seen her."

"Oh. Well, I'm sure she'll be here, Cathy . . ." They moved on, into the room. Toward the casket. Carl looked away.

He gritted his teeth. How could you do this, Anthony, he thought. What a stupidass thing to do, you son of a bitch! But Anthony had not been stupid. Never stupid! Pulled straight A's every single semester, except this last one . . . Played in tennis tournaments . . . Was on the swim team . . . God, the swim team!

Carl was on the swim team, too. Not a star like Anthony, but all right. And he'd had all he could do to keep his grades decent, forget about A's, with practice every day from four to six and sometimes mornings at six too. And weekends they had meets. Anthony breezed through it all. And he did . . . *this!* And if this could happen to Anthony, to him, to his family, what else could happen? If I'd known, he thought, I would have stopped you. Oh, yes. This never would have happened.

But how could he have known? . . .

The bus stop on East Mountain Road. Anthony sitting on the fence, just sitting, when he should have been coming home with Carl from afternoon swimming practice.

Carl turned the corner, jumped in surprise.

"Anthony?"

"Yeah."

"Man, you scared me! I didn't know who it was. Hey, where were you?"

"When?"

"Just now! Last two hours. We had practice, man!"

"I was here, Carly."

Carl put down his duffle and hoisted himself up on the fence next to Anthony. "Hey, Anthony, what's happening? What's wrong?"

Anthony turned toward him. "You, Carly. You're all wrong."

118

Carl frowned. "What do you mean?"

"You know, Carly, if you pull your arm like this, instead of like this . . ." Anthony did a swimming motion with the top of his torso, ". . . and you breathe like this, instead of like this, you'd shave about a tenth of a second off your time."

Carl laughed. "You're crazy, Anthony."

"I know," Anthony answered.

"Anyway, I'm talking about you. We need you. The team, I mean. We're no team without you, everyone knows that."

"Do me a favor, will you, cousin? Ask the coach to quit calling my mother, okay?"

"He won't quit calling. He wants to know what's the matter with you. So do I."

"Another thing, cousin, when you kick your feet, you—"

"Just shut up, Anthony. You know, you've been doing that all season. Not just to me, but to the other guys, too. Even Len Rosenthal mentioned it, and you know how much Len thinks of you! Telling everybody what they're doing wrong all the time, criticizing and all . . . You're worse than the coach and that's his job!"

Anthony blinked at him.

"I mean, everybody respects you Anthony, but you get so damn high and mighty, it's hard to even talk to you any more. And besides . . ." Carl slid off *the fence and picked up his duffle. ". . . You never say what anybody is doing right, only what we're doing wrong."*

"Oh, Carl, dear, I'm so sorry . . ." It was Mrs. Rossman, Carl's next-door neighbor.

"Yes. Thank you, Mrs. Rossman."

Carl leaned against the wall, out of the doorway where people had begun to brush against him.

At least he could have told me, he thought. He could have explained it or something so I—we— wouldn't feel so . . . so . . . Carl couldn't come up with the word and that made him angrier. I just can't stay here any more, he thought. I just can't! He craned his neck to find Ditto in the small crowd.

⇌

Rand stood before the closed wooden coffin at the end of the room. Out of the corner of his eye he saw that no one was near him, no one was watching . . . Ruth was talking to two women, her arm around Catherine whose head was down. Bill was . . . some- where. People were in the room, but it was as if they were there for other reasons. They didn't come near the coffin. Every now and then they would glance at it. It's closed, Rand thought almost angrily. You couldn't see my son anyway.

He touched the wood with both of his hands. He leaned against it.

"Anthony," he said under his breath. "Anthony."

He pushed at the coffin slightly, imagining it to be a cradle, imagining he were rocking it, rocking his son, rocking his baby . .

Tears started and they frightened him. He opened his eyes very wide and stepped back, making his body rigid, making fists. He took a deep breath and then another, until he felt in control.

He touched the coffin again. Not a cradle this time, but a boat. A large wooden rowboat, like the one they had rented a few weeks ago. To go fishing on Turtle Lake. . . .

He had fought with Catherine about Anthony's report card. They'd stayed up practically all Friday night . . . It had come in the mail that day, had greeted Rand on his return from Albany.

She wouldn't let him talk to Anthony until they'd discussed it together alone. He'd agreed, finally, and glared at his son all through the dinner which nobody ate except Denise.

"I think," Catherine said calmly when they were alone in his office, "that Anthony needs professional help, Rand."

"A psychiatrist?"

121

"Yes . . . or a psychologist . . . or a family counselor . . . somebody."

"Catherine, forget it." He made himself sound calm but he was seething. *Go to a shrink, that's today's answer to everything! He almost laughed thinking of his own father and what he would have thought of a shrink for his son! All kids are the same, do the same kid things, make the same kid mistakes, have the same kid aches and pains, and they get through it and get on with it! No! No shrink was going to take the responsibility out of his hands!*

"Rand, Anthony has not been himself for months."

"Catherine, this is the last I want to hear about this. You should have seen me when I was his age, you wouldn't have known me. Ecstatic one minute, kicking the dog the next. That's just plain growing up, Catherine. Believe me!"

"I want to—"

"Then do it. I know what I'm talking about. Listen, Cath, I love the boy. You know that. I wouldn't deprive him of anything I thought he really needed. I know what this is."

"Well, then . . . let's go to the school and talk to his teachers. Especially science and math. Rand, he failed them both! And he got a D in social studies! A boy who never got anything below a B in his life!"

"Catherine, I'm not going to that school. If I can't deal with my own son, then I just don't know what! Look. I agree, he's carrying this adolescent thing about as far as anyone can but I can handle it."

"All right," Catherine said, once she realized she'd never persuade him. "But why don't you try something different this time? I've yelled at him, you've yelled at him . . . Be calm, be nice to him. Get him to talk to you. Oh, Rand, take him to the lake! On Sunday! Take him fishing, he used to love that so!"

"It's almost November, Catherine . . ."

"It'll be all right, it's not that cold. You can dress warmly. Oh, please, Rand . . ."

He nodded. It was a good idea. Sure. Father and son. A good talk, they hadn't had one in a long time. The boy's all right. Hell, hadn't he had a few bad report cards in his day himself?

He'd spent Saturday with Catherine in the office, catching up on the week's work and phone messages he'd missed.

On Sunday, he and Anthony went to Turtle Lake and rented a rowboat.

"Want to row, Anthony?"

Anthony shook his head.

"Okay. I'll row."

They were fishing for bass. Rand had brought rubber worms and flatfish for bait. He'd always liked fishing, growing up in Michigan's Upper Peninsula, but when he was thirteen, his family had moved to California and he hadn't fished after that.

"I started fishing again when I was twenty," he said to Anthony, who didn't answer. "When I came east. Here. To New York. Didn't have much time. But every now and then I'd go." He stopped. Anthony was looking into the water. "Anthony . . . Here's your rod. You want to cast right over there. Into those weeds."

Anthony took the rod but he didn't cast.

"You know something? This time of year . . . I'm not even sure the bass season is still open." He cocked his head. "Could be illegal if we got one." He took his own rod and made a long cast, reeled in slowly. "But I think it runs through the first couple of weeks in November. I think."

Anthony looked at the reel and played with it.

"You're going to screw up your line, son. Go ahead, cast."

Anthony looked at him.

"Look, son . . . that report card really threw your mother and me . . ."

Anthony turned away.

"No, Anthony, look . . . don't do that, son . . . I want to understand here. I mean, what's happening with you? I'm your dad, I want to help. No, I do, really. Anthony, answer me."

124

"I can't," Anthony said. "I don't know what to say to you."

"Well, what about this report?"

"I don't know . . ."

"Anthony, you've got to do better than 'I don't know.' If something's on your mind, I want to know what it is."

Anthony looked down at the fishing rod and shrugged.

"You're not going to tell me?"

"I mean it," Anthony said softly. "I don't know what to say."

"Is it a girl? Is it that girl, that Czech girl?"

"No . . ."

"Something at school? The courses too dull? The teachers? Something happen with the swim team?"

"No . . ."

"Look, Anthony, I'm trying my best but you're no help. No help at all. Now let's have some answers. How can I do anything to help you if you won't help yourself! Now let's have it! Whatever it is!" He slammed his fishing rod against the side of the boat, breaking it. He cursed loudly.

"Oh, God, Anthony," Rand whispered to the closed wooden box. "I'm sorry." He leaned closer. "I didn't mean it . . . I just couldn't believe that my great kid had messed up . . . I didn't mean it . . ."

He started when he felt a hand on his shoulder.

It was his brother-in-law. "Come on over with us," Bill said.

Rand cleared his throat, turned his back to the crowd in the room. He couldn't look at Catherine, for fear she'd read his guilt, for fear he'd blurt it outright. He glanced at Bill.

"So many people here," he said and tried to smile.

⇌

In the small police station, Liz and Denise sat, sleepy-eyed and scared.

The policeman sat, looking at both of them, taking his time. "I can't call your parents," he said finally, "not with what they're going through. You." He pointed to Liz. "You get out of here. Go home. I catch you out of school again you're in big trouble. Understand?"

Liz nodded but hesitated, darting a look at Denise.

"Don't worry. I'll take care of her. Get going." The officer jerked his thumb at the door.

" 'Bye, Denise," Liz said.

" 'Bye."

"I'm very sorry about your brother . . . I saw him," the policeman said once Liz had left.

Denise nodded.

"I've got all this frightening stuff I could tell you about drugs . . . you must have gotten most of it in school . . ."

"Believe it!" she said and rolled her eyes.

"Yeah, and I can see it sure made an impression."

"Listen, I had my impressions made a long time ago," Denise answered.

"Well, your brother wasn't on anything, I know that."

She shook her head.

"What am I going to do with you, Denise?"

She smiled at him.

"Come on. I'll take you home. In my own car so your parents don't get scared." He stood up. "Well?" he said, looking down at the top of her head. "Come on."

⇌

Carl and Ditto walked slowly, stopping every now and then to kick or throw a stone, to lean against a tree, to retie a shoe that hadn't come untied. Carl had told his mother he was leaving—had to leave—and she'd understood, giving him a brief hug before he grabbed Ditto by the arm and pulled him outside.

They decided to go back to the Sheldon house, since no one would be home, but they weren't in a hurry to get there. Carl felt that being inside any building would make him choke. Even now he was panting, as if he had run a distance.

"Hey, where was Jana?" Ditto asked suddenly.

"I don't know. Wasn't she inside?"

"No. I didn't see her. I wonder where she went."

Carl stopped walking and began to swing around a street lamppost. He dug his heels into the dirt and let the momentum carry him—swinging fast, standing upright, dropping, swinging fast again.

"Maybe she was like me," he said. "Maybe she just couldn't stand being inside there."

"It's funny," Ditto said, "I was the one who didn't think I could make it, but once I was there, I felt a little better."

"I didn't."

"And where was Denise? I didn't see her at all."

"Bet you anything . . ." Carl stopped swinging and sat down on the curb, "Denise went out and got herself stoned somewhere. She'll probably come weaving in just as everybody's leaving."

"You think she'd do that? Today?"

"Don't you?"

"Nah. Not today."

"Bet you."

⇌

"You're pretty nice for a cop," Denise said, as they pulled up at her corner. "What's your name?"

"Lou Consiglia. I won't be so nice next time, Denise. That's a promise."

"That's a threat," she said.

He shrugged. "Okay, a threat then. As long as you get the message. I've really had it with seeing dead kids, Denise."

She looked down at her hands in her lap.

"You know just in this town there's at least one attempted suicide a month? By a kid?"

Denise shook her head.

"Doesn't that scare you?"

She didn't answer. Part of her was shocked. Part of her wasn't.

"It scares hell out of me," Consiglia said. "Most of them are attempts. Last couple of months—two successes. Your brother was one."

Now Denise looked at him.

"Yeah, that word? Successes? That's what they were, Denise. The kids succeeded. They achieved their goals. Is that your goal? You want to die, too?"

"Sometimes I guess I think about it," she said.

Consiglia put his arm on the back of the seat and swung around to face her. "Is that what you want for yourself? What Anthony chose?"

She was silent for a moment, then shook her head, no. "I don't know why, though. I really wonder if all the hassle is worth it."

"Because you have the hope that things will get better, don't you, Denise, no matter how bad they look? Your brother, and the others, believed that things would never, ever get better. It's like each of them was caught inside a tunnel, and they couldn't see any end to it or anything at all outside."

"Yeah," she said thoughtfully. Then she smiled. "Well, *do* things get better?"

"Sure," he said, smiling back. "And then they get worse, right? And then they get better again . . . Maybe sometimes they even get terrific!"

"I hope so," she said.

"That's the word."

For the first time, Denise noticed that her parents' Pontiac was in the garage. They're home, she thought. They're back. I'll have to go in there and face them.

"What time is it?" she asked.

"Three-thirty. Is that okay?"

"Yeah, it's just that I missed . . ." She stopped. She felt ashamed to tell him that she'd missed Anthony's wake. "Well . . ." She opened the car door. "Thanks for the ride."

"It's okay. Hang in there."

"Yeah, I will." She held her head up and walked to the front door.

Locked.

She frowned. Oh. They're not back. They went in

Uncle Bill's car. She reached behind the mailbox for the spare key and turned it in the lock. I'll just face them later, that's all, she thought. They'll just have to understand. I couldn't go, I just couldn't.

She opened the front door. The phone rang loudly and she jumped. "Damn!" she muttered, as she realized it was the office phone and ran for it.

The man on the other end started talking before she finished saying hello.

"Catherine, thank God you finally got home—I've been calling for over an hour—this is Bert from Kleinmann's in Rochester—is Rand there?"

Denise held the phone away from her ear for a moment. Her head was swimming. She thought: a business call for Daddy. All right. Take the message. You don't have to say anything to him.

She cleared her throat. "Excuse me, but this isn't—"

"Who's this, the daughter?"

"Yes . . ."

"Your mother not there? Or your father?"

"No."

An exasperated sigh at the other end. "Well, look, dear . . . when do you expect them?"

Denise pulled at the telephone wire. "I don't know . . ."

"Oh, God, is this my day," the caller moaned. "All

131

right, listen, honey, it's very important that your father call me the minute he gets in, you understand?"

"Yes," Denise said, and picked up a pencil. "Bert from . . ."

"Kleinmann's. Rochester. Now, look, dear, I want to tell you just what's happening so when he calls me back he'll have done something about it, okay?"

Denise swallowed and gripped the pencil.

"You hear me? Now listen . . ."

Denise wrote "new line, pre-Xmas sale" with a shaking hand. She couldn't keep up with what the man was saying and she hardly heard him.

". . . going to press tomorrow, the space is allocated and the window's empty . . ."

Denise said, "Allocated?"

"What?"

Denise rubbed her eyes. "What was 'allocated'? I didn't understand that last—"

"Damn it, I thought you kids were old enough! Look—"

Denise hung up.

The two chairs in Rand's office were piled with catalogues and papers, so Denise sat on the floor—sunk to the floor—as if her legs couldn't hold her up any longer.

That's what they do all the time, my father—and my mother—she thought. That's their life, allocate and substitute and pre-Christmas sale and I need it now. That's their life and Anthony doesn't have one any more and what am I doing with mine?

She heard the front door open but she realized she wasn't afraid. She walked out to meet them.

"Denise, thank heaven!" Ruth said, putting a hand up to her chest. "Honey, where were you?"

"I had to be by myself today, Aunt Ruth," Denise answered calmly.

Catherine blinked her eyes. "You should have told us," she said.

"I didn't want to wake you. I left very early."

"I was worried . . ."

Denise sighed. Good! she thought. "I'm going upstairs now," she said. Her father, who had been standing in the little entrance hall staring at nothing, looked up and nodded at her. She wasn't sure what he was nodding about. The telephone message was still in her hand. "Here," she said, holding it out to him. "Bert called. He said it was important."

Blankly, Rand took the paper and started for the office.

Denise turned and continued up the stairs.

⇌

Carl threw up in the kitchen of his house, and Ditto cleaned it up while Carl lay sobbing, his face pressed to the cold tile of the floor.

133

"It's okay, Carly—I mean, Carl," Ditto said help-lessly as he mopped, knowing it wasn't and feeling stupid.

Carl grew quiet after a while and lifted his head. There was a deep red ridge in his cheek from the edge of a tile. Ditto was sitting cross-legged on the floor next to him.

"What're *you* looking at," Carl grumbled.

"Nothing . . . You okay?"

"What are you, my manager? Just because you're manager of the swim team?"

"Aw, Carl . . ."

"Doesn't make you my *personal* manager, Ditto . . ."

"Okay, okay!"

"Yeah, manager of the swim team. That gave you a real big-man thing, didn't it, Ditto?"

"No, I just like to do it . . ."

"You know how Anthony begged and pleaded with the coach to give you that job?"

Ditto bit his lip.

"There were plenty of better guys for that job, but Anthony said he wouldn't swim unless you were manager. Did you know that, Dit?"

Ditto bit harder, tasting blood, and shook his head.

"Oh, yeah, 'If Henry Bonner doesn't manage, get

yourself another captain.' That's what he said, Ditto, and I know it because I was there!"

Now Ditto couldn't hold back the tears. Carl looked away. "Ditto," he finally said, "it's not you I'm mad at."

Ditto wiped his face with his sleeve. "Yeah. I guess I know. It's not you I'm cryin' at."

"Get me a glass of water, will you?" Carl asked.

Ditto rose instinctively and then sat back down. "Get it yourself," he said.

Carl laughed and stood up. He was suddenly unbearably thirsty.

"Carl?" Ditto asked.

"Yeah?"

"Did you talk to Anthony about the way he was? You know . . . See, I thought it was just me, I didn't really think maybe it was Anthony . . ."

Carl finished his water and ran some more from the tap. "I tried to, but he turned me off. Anyway, I kept figuring he'd get over it."

Ditto said, "Yeah . . ."

"Sorry I said all that before," Carl mumbled.

"It's okay."

"Listen . . . thanks for cleaning up the mess."

Ditto couldn't answer. His eyes had filled again. He wondered if he would ever stop crybabying over any little thing! But the phone rang suddenly and when Carl turned to answer it, Ditto blinked hard and pinched the skin on his arm until he was safe. He wouldn't cry now and Carl hadn't seen.

"Hello? . . . Yeah, hi, Mom . . . Yeah . . . Yeah . . . No, I'm not alone, Ditto's here . . . No, you don't have to . . . Yeah, I'm all right, I swear . . . Okay . . . O-*kay*, I will . . . Yeah . . . 'Bye." Carl hung up, sighed, and turned back to Ditto. "Hey, Dit, you have to go home soon?"

"I guess so. Why?"

"Because when you do I have to go back to Anth—back to my aunt's house. My mother doesn't want me to be alone." He laughed. "You believe that? She thinks I'm three years old!" Suddenly he was hungry. Starving. "Hey, Ditto, let's heat up some frozen pizza, okay?" he said. He was smiling.

⇌

In his office, Rand stood against his desk and leaned heavily on it with his knuckles. Twice he had picked up the telephone to call Rochester and twice he had not even dialed. He turned around as Catherine came into the room.

"Are you all right?" she asked.

"Yes . . ."

She looked at the message on the desk. "Did you call Bert?"

"No."
She nodded slowly.

⇌

Alone in her room with the door closed, Denise sat on her bed, twisting the hem of her pillowcase, sliding its edges between her fingers, bunching it up in her fist, relaxing, then twisting again.

"I don't believe it, Anthony!" she said out loud. "I don't believe you did it!"

Officer Lou Consiglia's face appeared in her mind. He talked to her the way Anthony used to . . . sympathetically, with humor. She liked that. She liked *him*. She smiled. Then stopped. How could she smile, her brother was dead . . .

Anthony! It was always Anthony this and Anthony that, Anthony's grades, Anthony's sports, Anthony always listened and always obeyed. Denise, our little baby, she's a girl so what can she do? At least if she were good in school or at least if she were *pretty* or something . . .

No, she thought. Stop it, that's not fair. Let's be fair, now. Daddy never said that, he never did. Then why have I always felt it?

I'm fat, she said to herself. I never cared about school, I never was any good at sports—she laughed: a short bark, a cough—and God knows, I never listened!

I did care about school, though . . . but it was just so hard, with all the teachers saying, so you're *Anthony's* little sister, well, we just expect great things from *you* . . .

"Oh, Anthony, *I* should have done it, not you!" she cried to the wall . . .

"Come on, Anthony, no! No, you can't get out of the water yet, not till you get it right! Don't go away, Denise, you're next. Now: take a breath, face in. Face to the side, breathe out. Again. Breathe in, face in. Roll your face to the side, breathe out. Again."

"Rand? It's getting chilly . . ."

"In a minute, Catherine, I want the kids to be water-safe!"

"Well, they can learn to be water-safe tomorrow, too . . ."

"Tomorrow we learn the back float. I want to work on their breathing today."

"I'm cold, Daddy . . ."

"Look, Anthony, you'll thank me when you're the best little swimmer on this beach, right?" He smiled at his son. "Come on, sonny, for me. Okay?"

"Okay!"

"Atta boy!"

Five-year-old Denise touched the water with her toe. She felt goose bumps over her shoulders and arms. She eyed her father, who was concentrating on

138

Anthony, and very slowly she backed away from the water's edge. Back, back, back until she reached a clump of trees and a picket fence. She immediately ducked down, knowing she couldn't be seen from the beach.

Denise moved from her bed to the mirror, leaned over the vanity table and thrust her face close to the glass. She touched her cheeks, forehead, turning her head this way, that way. Two zits here, she observed. Gorgeous, Denise, a real Miss America. Look at your hair. Sell it for twine in any hardware store.

She sat down on the vanity stool.

She made a face at herself. "But you've got guts," she whispered to the Denise in the mirror. "You never said 'yes, Daddy' all the time if you thought he was full of it like Anthony used to. You stood up to him . . . And to Mom, too. Wish I had a nickel for every time she said, 'Oh, Denise, I just wish you had some of your brother's determination' or 'Oh, Denise, I just wish you could apply yourself to your responsibilities like your brother does.'" She stood up, jammed her fingers into her jeans pockets. She felt Liz's pills in their plastic bag. I don't need these, she told herself, I'll throw them out. She squeezed the bag. No, it's stupid to waste them.

She dropped the bag into the vanity drawer.

"Denise?"

She jumped. Carl was standing in her doorway.

"Hi, Carl," she said softly. "Did you just get here? I didn't even hear the doorbell . . ."

"Yeah," he said and shifted his weight from one foot to the other.

"Come on in," Denise sighed. "I'm really glad to see you . . ."

Carl sat down on the edge of the bed. Denise turned to face him. They didn't speak.

$$\rightleftharpoons$$

Catherine and Ruth in the kitchen: one at the refrigerator, one at the stove stirring Campbell's tomato soup slowly in a metal pan. Every now and then their eyes met.

"Cathy, does Rand know about the ties?"

"God, no."

"You're not telling him then."

"No. Would you?"

"I don't know . . . Probably not. What good would it do."

"Ruth . . . what do you think Anthony meant by doing that? The ties, I mean . . ."

"I don't know, Cathy."

"Do you think he was saying his father killed him or something? That he hated his father?"

"I'm not a psychiatrist, Cathy . . ."

140

"But it must have meant something . . . I keep thinking about what must have been in his mind those last few hours when I wasn't with him . . ."

"I think it was in his mind long before those last few hours, Cathy."

"Oh, Ruth," Catherine moaned, "I tried to get him to a psychiatrist." . . .

"Rand, we've got to get some help for Anthony!"

"Yes? What kind of help?"

"Psychiatric."

"Goddamn it, Catherine, don't start that again."

"He's changed, Rand. And it's getting worse, not better. I know because I'm home all the time . . ."

"Lower your voice. The kids will hear you."

"Randolph, the kids are more than aware of what's going on. You're the one who won't face it!"

"Listen to me, Catherine, for the last time. You were never a fifteen-year-old boy. You don't know what it's like. I do. Anthony's perfectly normal and he'll get over it."

"I'm not sure any more," she said softly. "He's given up swimming, tennis, he cuts school, he won't see his friends . . . even Jana. And look at him, Rand . . . I don't even know the last time he took a shower. His clothes . . ." her voice trailed.

"He'll be all right, Catherine!" Rand yelled. "We've got to get his mind on something besides him-

self, that's all. I'll buy him one of those new cal-
culators. He'll love it. Figuring things out . . .
That'll do it. I'll get him something like that. What do
you think?"

"Rand—I'm frightened."

"Cathy, it'll be all right. We can handle Anthony.
I mean, we've done okay for fifteen years, haven't
we?"

"Catherine," Ruth said, "don't torture yourself
now. Look . . . lots of people see psychiatrists and
still kill themselves. We just don't know. And we
never will. So you can go on saying 'If I'd only done
this or that' but it won't do any good, so we've just
got to pick up and go on. You've still got Denise to
think about. I've got Carl . . ." She went to her sister
and put her arms around her. "Listen. Maybe he was
using the ties to get *closer* to his father. To reach out
to him one last time. It could be that, huh?"

Catherine shook her head against Ruth's shoulder. "I don't know . . ."

"Well, it could be. You could look at it a lot of
ways, Cathy. Cathy?"

"What?"

"Did you read Anthony's stories?"

"Which stories?"

"Any of them. When he was writing so much. Did
you read them?"

142

"Whenever he gave them to me. Why?"

Ruth gently took her sister's face between her hands. "Because I think maybe it will help a little if you read them again. Those are Anthony's real last words and maybe they will help us understand. And if they don't do that, at least they'll bring us just a little closer to him. And we'll always have them."

⇌

"Ruth, would it be okay if Carl sits in front with me?" Bill asked.

The Sheldons were standing at their car in the Hamils' driveway. They had finished another quiet dinner at which not much was eaten. It was dark and all three thought it was much later than it actually was.

"Of course," Ruth answered. Bill pushed the seat forward and Ruth slid into the back.

Bill didn't say anything until they reached the end of the block and turned left toward home. Then he cleared his throat and half-turned to his son.

"Carl?"

"Yeah?"

"I just want to say that . . . that if you've got something—anything—on your mind, well, I want you to know that you can . . . come to us with it."

Carl looked at him.

143

"What I mean is, son, we *want* you to come to us. Your mother and I. We don't want you to feel like, like you're all alone, with nobody to—to care. Am I making myself clear?"

Carl look at his father. "Daddy?"

Bill said, "Yeah?" at the same time it occurred to him that Carl hadn't called him "Daddy" in years.

"What you said about being all alone. I guess that's . . . I think that's what I've been feeling."

"We all feel that," Ruth said from the back seat. "We feel alone when a friend does something . . . that shocks us. Or surprises us. We all feel unsure. Of ourselves. Of everything."

Carl sighed. "Yeah."

"Well . . ." Bill said, finally, looking straight ahead. "Your mother and I . . . we just want you to know . . . we care about you, son."

Ruth did not wipe her tears. "You can be sure of that, Carl," she said.

Carl rubbed his eyes and nodded. I love you, too, he said inside.

⇌

Changing into pajamas. Washing up. Nighttime rituals.

Bill Sheldon, home now, thinking: I saw Rand's face at Anthony's coffin. It could have been me, it could have been Carl. I'll never forget that look on Rand's face . . . But he didn't mention his thought to Ruth . . .

Ditto Bonner, curled up in a ball in his bed at eight-thirty, the lights out, his eyes wide open . . .

Anthony's swim team and the coach, having gotten permission to use the school pool late this evening, doing laps until they were exhausted . . .

Liz Keyserling, calling her friends, getting stoned, telling them all about her crazy day . . .

Denise, looking down at her body in a tub of hot water, deciding to diet, wondering if Anthony would have been proud of her, wondering what did go on in Anthony's mind . . .

Rand and Catherine, undressing slowly in their bedroom, avoiding each other's eyes, presence . . .

Jana Zenek, sleeping at last, dreaming of twin boys, playing happily with a white dog . . .

Walter Pratt, at his writing desk, rereading Anthony's essay "On Peace" and thinking, do I really understand kids? Have I ever understood *any* of them?

Off-duty Officer Lou Consiglia, in a bar with Fred Rudell, asking what more he could possibly say to a kid like Denise Hamil that wouldn't sound autocratic and preachy the way all adults had sounded to him when he was a kid . . .

And Carl Sheldon, sleeping soundly, dreaming nothing, with his thumb in his mouth . . .

7

$\rightleftharpoons$

Morning.

Anthony's essay was still on Walter Pratt's desk. The teacher folded it neatly and put it in his pocket. Yesterday at the funeral home, he had asked Catherine if he might read something at the service and she had nodded and touched his hand. His thought was to offer Anthony's "On Peace," but remembering his conversation with the boy, he decided it would not be an appropriate thing to do. He chose instead a poem by Lew Sarett: "The Sheepherder." Anthony had once read it aloud in class and now it seemed particularly significant. All that responsibility on the sheepherder's shoulders, or so he felt . . . More and more sheep to care for . . . and all his . . . the sheepherder could see nothing else in his world . . .

Pratt decided to bring Anthony's essay with him and give it to the parents. Perhaps Anthony would have objected to that, too, but they were his people. They were entitled to it. The teacher picked up the little book of poems and left his apartment.

⇌

Jana leaned against the edge of her bed and looked out her window. A cloud was sitting on the little duck pond the Corbins had dug and filled before Jana and her grandfather had come to The Rosetrees. The sky was overcast again. It would probably rain.

Jana had on a black skirt and sweater. The skirt was cotton and she knew she would probably be cold, but it was the only black skirt she had.

Her night had been peaceful and she felt guilty that she had slept well. She thought she owed it to Anthony now to think about New York. She wished she'd had the courage to tell him at the pond instead of running . . .

She and her grandfather had lived in the city almost a year. She had gone to school. A big brick and glass building that probably wasn't very old but looked as if it were. It was dirty. The city was dirty. The language was strange. But it was a new place, different. Jana found it exciting because she wanted to and because her grandfather had told her she didn't have to be afraid any more.

So she hadn't been afraid the night she went out to the bakery. Děda had said he would go but she had insisted. They would have rolls with their soup. Big, fat puffy ones with seeds like the ones she had loved at home. You can get everything in this city, she'd

147

told him, all kinds of foods from every country in the world!

She'd run out, skipping like a little girl, even though she was big, almost thirteen, and when the boy stopped her on her way home, she hadn't thought to be afraid. Until he touched her. He pulled her between two buildings, a small alley, and down some cement steps into a well outside a basement doorway. The door was locked; she had tried it, wresting her body away from him for an instant, too terrified to scream. He grabbed at her, pulling her down, tearing her skirt, covering her mouth with his hand. He never said a word while he ripped her in half. She was sure that's what he was doing. It wasn't like being cut with a knife, it was like being torn in two. A knife would be swift, this was slow, so slow and with more pain than she felt it was possible to endure.

And after he had ripped her in two, he had left, pulling and zipping at his pants, running up the stone steps without looking back. She lay in the well watching him, a paper bag under her feet and the big puffy rolls scattered over the cement.

There were police. Many of them, but not at once. First there was a lady, a fat lady with a torn coat, she was coming down the steps of the well and then she ran back up again, so fast for a fat lady, lumbering up the steps as Jana watched her . . . She was back in a minute with a policeman, he talked at her, she didn't answer. Then there was the hospital car, a screaming siren, the policeman in there with her, talking at her, she couldn't answer him . . .

A hospital. Lying there in a hall, waiting, waiting, sleeping, waiting . . . A policewoman came, then doctors came. They talked at her, too, most of their talk she didn't understand, they put her in a room, poked at her with the noses of big machines, hurt her again, hurt her *there* again . . .

She began to cry, to cry with all her heart.

Then there were more policemen. Different ones. They wanted her to tell them things. They pushed at her with their voices: press charges, charges . . . she kept shaking her head: no, no, go away, go away . . .

And they did. They went away and left her alone. The doctors were finished with her and they left her alone. She stopped crying.

The policewoman helped her home. Děda had been frantic. He cried when he saw her, tried to hold her but she pulled free. She told him she'd been hurt.

She stayed on her bed for days. She wouldn't go out, wouldn't go to school. Finally, she got up to do small chores. I'll clean, she thought. I'll cook what Děda brings home. But I won't go out, even into the hall.

After two months, Děda had gotten them their

jobs at The Rosetrees and moved them away, out of New York City forever. She never found out how he did it. She never asked. She never talked about New York again and she never let him touch her.

"Janička?"

"Yes?"

"A young man is here . . ."

Jana turned away from the window. "Young man?"

Her grandfather nodded once and held his arm out toward the front room. "One who came yesterday . . ."

Ditto. In a too-small suit. He stood shyly near the front door.

"What happened yesterday, Jana?" he asked her as they walked together. "Did I say something wrong?"

"No . . . It's . . . just that I can't help thinking that it was somehow my fault what happened." She surprised herself by saying it to Ditto so calmly. But then, he had surprised her by coming there for her, to get her, to be with her. It was something that Anthony would have done.

"That's what we all think, Jana," Ditto said. She stopped walking and looked at him. "At least Carl and I do. I mean, we think we should have known something was wrong, a lot more wrong than we figured

. . . He talked about it, suicide, at least a couple of times to both of us and we just passed it off."

"When did he talk about it? When?"

"As far back as last summer, Jana."

"Really? That is the truth, Ditto? That far?"

"Honest."

"He never spoke of it to me," she said after a pause.

"You know, the day before he died," Ditto said, turning toward her as they walked, "I really thought everything was terrific. Did you see him? Yeah, you said you did in the afternoon . . ."

"Yes, in the afternoon. But only for a few minutes. He did seem fine. He smiled at me. He said he'd had an excellent English class. He said he had much work to do and would do it after school. He smiled at me . . ."

Ditto nodded as she spoke. "Yeah. He told me that, too. And he had on clean clothes . . . I guess he'd been pretty grubby for a while there, but I didn't really realize it until I saw him looking so cool that day, you know?"

"Yes, I know. I noticed too."

"I felt so good, Jana . . . Anthony was coming back, I thought. Everything was nice . . . That's what Anthony said. That everything felt nice. Good again. I don't get it, Jana. I don't get it."

Jana glanced sidelong at him. I cannot tell him, she thought. I cannot tell him how much is my fault. But I must make a confession to Anthony's family. I must do it because I ran away and now Anthony's dead.

⇌

Denise stood in the hall by herself. Her parents and the Sheldons had gone into a small room next to the chapel, where they would sit, receiving visitors, until the service began.

People began to arrive. Carl came out to bring Denise into the receiving room to stand by her parents. She stood next to her mother, glancing now and then at her father. Rand stood up to shake Sanford Pound's hand. He seemed composed. He looked thin in his dark suit.

Catherine was seated. Her eyes were dry. She looked up and nodded now and then, as someone offered a sympathetic word. The Sheldons nodded, too. Tight-lipped and somber they stood together behind the Hamils' chairs.

The Bonners arrived, with Ditto's sister. The crowd in the receiving room drifted. The swim team came in a group, Denise noticed. One of them, Len Rosenthal, kissed her mother on the cheek. The sight made Denise's eyes fill. There were lots of kids from school . . . Liz, Lacey, even scuzzy Stevie! And teachers . . .

After a while, the men moved off together to one side, the women to another. Were they talking about Anthony? she wondered. About her and her parents? Or recipes and golf games, children and the stock market, clothes and business, money and the weather and TV and the energy crisis and the championship fight . . .

She slipped out again, into the hall, where she found Jana and Ditto standing together.

"Hi," she whispered to them.

Ditto said, "Hi, Denise. Where's Carl?"

"In there," Denise motioned.

Jana drew in her breath. Denise! she thought. She would tell Denise. No matter what, she would tell Denise. She would confess her blame to Anthony's sister. Then Anthony's family would know her responsibility in the death of their son, which they had every right to know.

"Ditto, you go inside and find Carl," she said. "I must talk with Denise alone."

"Oh," he answered. "Sure. Okay." He disappeared into the crowd.

"What, Jana?" Denise asked. Never had Jana begun a conversation with her. Never. "What is it?"

"I have something to tell you which is painful, Denise, but it is about—"

"They're starting," Carl said from the doorway of the chapel. "You have to come in now."

Ditto appeared again at Jana's side.

"Afterward, Jana," Denise said. "We'll talk later. All right?"

Jana nodded.

She didn't hear the poem by Lew Sarett that Walter Pratt read or the swimming coach's eulogy or Len Rosenthal's selections by Alan Watts or the tribute by the high school principal. Her head was swimming with alternate feelings of terror and relief and what she would tell Anthony's sister.

Carl didn't hear the service either. He wanted to remember Anthony. The Anthony he had known so well, not the one lying up there in a box. That Anthony he didn't know at all.

The last night. The night before he died. A phone call . . .

"Carl? Hey, can you come over, Carly?"

"Anthony? Sure! Sure, gimme five!" And he raced out of his room, leaving the desk light burning over six pages of math, an English theme and a half-finished map of North America.

And there was Anthony, waiting on his front steps. Smiling.

"Hey, look at you," Carl said teasingly. "Your hair's even combed!"

154

Anthony laughed. "I know," he said, "I'm beautiful."

They sat down on the steps. It was a warm night, Carl noticed. Or maybe it was just the way he was feeling. Anthony really looked so good, so different . . .

"I left a pile of homework, cuz, but it was worth it."

Anthony smiled and clapped him on the shoulder. "I feel good, Carly," he said. "Boy, did I work today. My father won't believe my room! It looks like the Hilton Hotel. Gorgeous! Did stuff for school like you wouldn't believe! I think I caught up on everything."

Carl shook his head in awe. "In one afternoon you caught up on like two month's worth of work . . . And I can't even catch up from yesterday! You know the crazy thing? I believe you!"

"Yeah, well, not everything, but all the important stuff. And while I was working on analyzing this poem for English, I got a great idea for a story. Wham! So I drafted it up," Anthony explained excitedly. "There's this magazine I used to subscribe to and it publishes short stories by unknowns. I know the kind of thing they like."

"Hey, great, Anthony."

"Miss me on the swim team?"

"You kidding?"

"We're gonna have the fastest team any high

school has ever had, Carly. How will it feel to be a member of the fastest high school swim team that was ever in existence!"

"Boy, will it be good to have you back," Carl said. "Ol' Len will probably have a party or something."

"He's a good guy, Len," Anthony said. "Yeah. A good guy. Say, Carly, you hungry?"

Carl felt his fists clench in his lap. Anger again. It swept over him in waves and he could feel the sweat on his neck and under his arms.

He looked at his mother and his father. They glanced back briefly. His armpits were wet. He wanted to run again, bolt again as he'd done yesterday, but he knew he couldn't. He wanted to scream, *He lied to me, he lied to me!* but instead he concentrated all his efforts on not being sick there in the pew in front of everyone . . .

⇌

"It was a nice service."

"Quiet . . . you could hear a pin drop."

"Funny, they didn't have Reverend Bellwood."

"Maybe he wouldn't do it because of the, you know, the circumstances."

"Oh, don't be silly, Velma."

"The poetry was nice . . ."

156

"Parents are holding up remarkably well, don't you think?"

Denise listened to all of it as people from the town filed past her. You'd think they'd know I'm standing right here . . .

"Hi, Denise."

She looked up dully to see Liz Keyserling and Roddy Pound.

"Hi, Liz."

"You stoned?"

"No . . ."

"Roddy and I are meeting some kids behind the school. Want to come?"

Denise shook her head.

"Want me to come over later?"

"No."

"You sure? Okay, then. See you."

"Uh, 'bye, Denise," Roddy Pound said to the floor. And he and Liz disappeared.

"Denise?"

She turned. "Yes, Mom . . ."

"Your father and I . . . and your aunt and uncle . . . We're going to the crematory . . ."

"Yes."

"Will you come with us?" It was a ride, twenty miles away.

"I think maybe I'll go home. Maybe some people will come . . . Mom? Are you all right?" Denise

157

moved to grab her mother's arm. Catherine seemed to be sinking and Rand was still inside. "Come here, Mom . . ." Denise helped her mother back into Archway's. Somehow she found the ladies' room. Catherine almost fell into a chair near the sink. Denise wet some paper towels and put them up against her mother's forehead. Suddenly Catherine began to sob.

"Oh, God, Denise, if I had just taken him off to a doctor back in the beginning . . ."

"Mom . . . Mommy . . ."

"No, no, let me, if I had listened to Ruth back last summer, 'way back then, Denise, but you know what? You know what?" She'd stopped crying and her eyes were glowing. "I fought with your father about it but in the end I was glad. I was glad he said what he said. I didn't want to believe Anthony was that bad off. Denise, I wanted to believe your father. It was my fault, it was."

"No, Mom, it was Daddy's fault!" She drew a breath. "Daddy was never home, he was never around, he left everything up to you and then when you tried to do something he'd come home like some visitor and tell you not to. He made Anthony do all those sports—"

"Oh, no, Denise, Anthony wanted to do those things—"

"To please Daddy, that's why!"

"Oh, my little girl," Catherine said, touching Denise's cheek. "It isn't that simple . . ."

The door to the ladies' room opened and Mrs. King from the library came in. Surprised to be confronting the family in such close quarters, she didn't know whether to leave or stay.

"So sorry, Catherine," she managed in a hushed tone. "So sorry, Denise. I—I'll come back when you're finished, I didn't mean to interrupt, I'm . . . so sorry . . ."

"Denise," Catherine said, once the automatic door had closed again, "your father loved Anthony. He loves you."

Denise looked away.

"And *I* love you." Catherine tried to smile, though her eyes were streaming again. "Have I told you that lately?"

$$\rightleftharpoons$$

Jana and Ditto and Denise and Carl went back to the Hamils' by themselves. Carl hadn't wanted to come, though his nausea had passed. But he hadn't wanted to go to the crematory either, and Ruth insisted that she didn't want him to be alone. After making everyone promise that Carl would stay with them, Anthony's parents, his aunt and his uncle drove off in the limousine that Archway's provided.

Denise took Jana upstairs to her room. Ditto stayed downstairs with Carl, wanting to be useful.

"Hey, Carl?" he began because Carl had not said anything for five minutes.

"What."

"You want to throw something? You want to yell at me? Listen, it's okay." Ditto sat down on the couch and braced himself.

"He lied to me that last night, Ditto," Carl said suddenly, viciously. "He made *plans* with me, talked about the *future* with me, he *conned* me, because all the time he knew that the next morning he'd be dead and none of it would happen and he would never explain to me *why!*"

Ditto looked at him. He squinted his eyes. He didn't know what to say.

"Don't you see? Wouldn't you be mad? If you were taken in that way? Wouldn't you feel like the prime sucker of the universe? If Anthony could do that to me, then how am I supposed to know what's going to happen ever? It makes me sick!"

Ditto licked his lips. "Hey. Maybe he didn't know then. Maybe he really did plan those things, Carl. Maybe he meant them . . ."

"Yeah, and less than twelve hours later he kills himself? He *lied!*"

"I don't know, I don't know," Ditto said quickly. "But you have to remember, he wasn't like himself,

160

Carl. Remember that. We talked about it. He wasn't like himself to Jana either, or to me. Or in school or anything, Carl! So don't judge him by that last night. You can't, see? Because it wasn't our Anthony then. Carl?"

Carl began to rock on his heels back and forth. "But he *was!* That night he *was,* Ditto!"

"No. He really wasn't. Because of what he did. See, maybe he came out of it just for that time, just for a little time. But not for real. Because our Anthony never would've, Carl. He never would've. Something got him and we don't know what it was but he didn't lie on purpose, Carl. I'd bet on it, I would." Ditto shook his head for emphasis.

Carl stopped rocking and looked down at his shoes. "Maybe," he said. "Maybe. Hey, Ditto, do you think—what you just said—maybe we could ask somebody about it? Like the psychologist at school? Because it makes sense, you know, that the Anthony we grew up with, he wouldn't lie like that, he wouldn't make it like some horrible trick he was playing, do you think we could, Dit?"

"Oh, yeah," Ditto nodded. "We should do that. Let's do that."

"Tomorrow," Carl said.

"Tomorrow."

⇌

"Jana . . ." Denise said, after the girl had told her in one sentence, it one breath, about Anthony at the pond. ". . . Do you think Anthony killed himself because you wouldn't let him touch you? Is that your confession?"

"Yes, because you see, he was so hurt and I ran away and we didn't talk at all after that except the day before . . ." Jana forced herself to keep looking into Denise's face. She waited for Denise to scream at her, even hit her. Or call the boys so that everyone could see who was to blame for all their grief. But Denise just sat down dully on her bed.

"Oh, Jana, people don't kill themselves just because some girl says no. Do they?" Jana didn't answer. "Do they do that in Czechoslovakia?"

Jana shook her head.

"Well they don't do it here, either. Unless they're crazy or something. And Anthony wasn't crazy. He felt lousy, that's for sure, but he wasn't crazy. And now you say it's your fault, my mother thinks it's her fault, I've been thinking it's my father's fault, and . . . oh, Jana, *that's* maybe what's crazy . . ."

Jana said, "Ditto thinks it's his fault."

"*Ditto!*"

"He said he and Carl should have recognized signals that Anthony was giving them. And they never did."

"Oh, God, oh God, me, too, Jana. The trophies,

162

the way he cut school, the way he suddenly got off my case, I was glad and sorry he did that . . . That time in his room . . . I told him I knew how he felt. I really thought I did, Jana, I thought I was so smart, I knew just how he felt. But I didn't know at all."

Jana's lip quivered. "I think nobody did," she whispered.

Denise looked up at her. "Well who *is* to blame then, Jana?"

⇌

In the evening, the swim team came by with the coach, who kept asking softly, "Do you think I pushed him too hard? Do you think I was too hard on him maybe?" Walter Pratt was there, pressing the original copy of Anthony's essay, folded into squares, into Catherine's hand. Mrs. Sanford Pound came with her daughter Lacey. She left a coffee cake. The high school principal came with his wife, bringing a box of chocolates. The Bonners came, said Ditto could stay as long as he was needed. Rand's widowed sister-in-law called from California.

Ditto and Denise handled it all. Denise made coffee and Ditto got the cups and trays. Ditto answered the door and the phone. Denise cut up the Pounds' coffee cake and got out plates. Ditto washed dishes. They took turns making sure that Jana didn't sit too long alone in a corner by assigning her little tasks. They tried to draw Carl in but stopped when they saw he was content to stay with his father. They didn't notice when Rand and Catherine went upstairs.

"We're going, Dit," Carl said finally as Ditto passed him carrying a tray of plates.

Ditto put the tray on a table. "Yeah. Okay, Carl."

"You want a lift home?"

"Thanks, but I'll stay. Help Denise clear up. You know, just . . . be here a while."

"I'll see you in school, Dit . . ."

"Yeah, Carl. See you in school."

When Len Rosenthal left at ten-thirty, they found they were alone together, the three of them; a short, skinny boy looking more eleven than fifteen; a tall plump girl with stringy hair; a smaller, frail-looking girl in a black wool sweater and black cotton skirt.

They stayed by the door for a minute after it closed, looking at each other. Then Ditto reached out with both his arms, toward the girls. Denise stepped into them quickly and with a little sob, she hugged him, tight and hard. Then they turned toward Jana. Their arms outstretched, they went to her. All three of them held onto each other.

$$\rightleftharpoons$$

"A baby bird falls out of its nest. It has flown before, it can't understand. Suddenly its wings refuse to move. The air, which had always felt so welcome, is an enemy. Above, his parents fly in circles, squawking at him. He can't understand what they're trying to tell him. He only knows he can't move his wings. He feels his heart pounding. His beak is open and his little tongue is sticking out. There is no part of his body he can control. He stays this way for a long time. Hours. Maybe longer.

"Suddenly he is moving! He is soaring! He isn't doing it himself, he isn't moving his wings, something is doing it for him! Nothing hurts, there is no pain, and he is flying higher, much higher than he has ever flown, higher than his parents have ever flown!

"He doesn't see his parents any more but he knows they are happy for him. They couldn't stay there, above him, watching his pain. Now they know his pain is gone. He feels glorious, free! Soon he can see the outline of the earth below. He never knew how small it was.

"Death can not be grim. It is like a soft, warm blanket on a winter night. It wraps itself all around, keeping out wind and bad voices. Death can be a piece of luck. It should be celebrated.

"When my grandmother died I felt sad for a long time, but I don't any more. We were all there when she said goodbye, and I cried. When I had stopped crying, I still felt as if I were, even though there weren't any tears. It wasn't until much later that I began to feel good about my grandmother.

"There we were, gathered around her as she left us. It was as if we had cut the moorings on a cloud-boat, at last allowing it to drift off on its own, floating down a never-ending river of stars; and the rest of us, remaining, must surely celebrate that for her the ties to earthly anguish are broken forever and she is free.

"This must be the best peace there is."

Catherine stopped reading and looked up. Rand was lying on his back on the bed, his hands locked together over his stomach.

"Rand?"

"Mmm?"

"Were you listening?"

"I was listening."

"Rand, he called it 'On Peace.' "

"I know."

"Mr. Pratt said that Anthony was angry that it was read in class without his permission. That's why

Mr. Pratt didn't read it today . . . but he wanted us to have it . . ."

"I don't understand, Catherine. I don't understand, I don't understand. I have so many questions . . . and I don't even know if I'd understand the answers. If there are any answers . . ."

"Why did Anthony believe that death was the only kind of peace he could find?" Catherine said. She sat down next to him on the bed. He moved over for her and she covered his hands with her own. "I don't know either, Rand," she whispered, and put her face down on their folded hands.

Also by Fran Arrick
Steffie Can't Come Out to Play